Charlotte Parks was every bit as beautiful as the last time Brando had seen her, naked in his bed, her long golden hair splayed across the pillow, her mouth swollen from his kisses.

This morning she looked impossibly self-contained, as well as impossibly glowing. Pregnancy suited her. Her skin appeared more luminous, her eyes bluer, brighter, her long golden-blond hair shimmering in the sunlight that poured through the tall windows.

When Louisa had come upstairs to tell him there was a woman at the door, demanding to see him, he'd arched a brow but hadn't been concerned. When he'd discovered it was Charlotte in the salon, he'd been intrigued. Charlotte, fascinating Charlotte, never made demands, and yet she'd been pure pleasure in his bed. But now he wasn't as sanguine. Apparently, she was pregnant. With his child.

New York Times and *USA TODAY* bestselling author **Jane Porter** has written forty romances and eleven women's fiction novels since her first sale to Harlequin in 2000. A five-time RITA® Award finalist, Jane is known for her passionate, emotional and sensual novels, and loves nothing more than alpha heroes, exotic locations and happily-ever-afters. Today Jane lives in sunny San Clemente, California, with her surfer husband and three sons. Visit janeporter.com.

Books by Jane Porter

Harlequin Presents

Bought to Carry His Heir
The Prince's Scandalous Wedding Vow
Christmas Contract for His Cinderella

Conveniently Wed!

His Merciless Marriage Bargain

The Disgraced Copelands

The Fallen Greek Bride
His Defiant Desert Queen
Her Sinful Secret

Passion in Paradise

His Shock Marriage in Greece

Stolen Brides

Kidnapped for His Royal Duty

Visit the Author Profile page
at Harlequin.com for more titles.

Jane Porter

THE PRICE OF A DANGEROUS PASSION

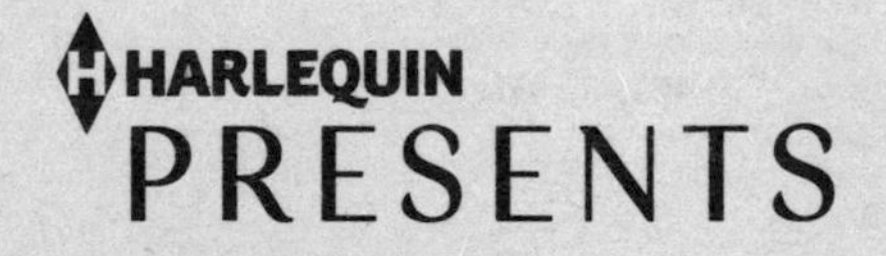

HARLEQUIN® PRESENTS®

Recycling programs for this product may not exist in your area.

ISBN-13: 978-1-335-14877-3

The Price of a Dangerous Passion

This edition published by arrangement with Harlequin Books S.A.

For questions and comments about the quality of this book, please contact us at CustomerService@Harlequin.com.

Harlequin Enterprises ULC
22 Adelaide St. West, 40th Floor
Toronto, Ontario M5H 4E3, Canada
www.Harlequin.com

Printed in U.S.A.

THE PRICE OF A DANGEROUS PASSION

For my editor, Megan Haslam,
so good to have you back!
You're a dream to work with.

PROLOGUE

New Year's Eve

SHE HAD RULES. Rules she never broke. There were no exceptions. Charlotte never mixed business and pleasure, never. She wasn't ever tempted, either… regardless of the value of her clients. All her clients were VIPs to her, clients who came to her for her sterling reputation. They trusted her to make the best possible decisions for them. They came to her because they needed her expertise in sorting out image issues, public relation snafus and social media nightmares. How could they trust her judgment, if her judgment was faulty?

If her judgment lost sight of the objective?

If she forgot why she was there in the first place?

Charlotte Parks knew all these things, and yet Brando Ricci was making it almost impossible to remember why these—*her*—rules were so important. She'd wrapped up business weeks ago, well before Christmas. All conversations and concerns with the Ricci-Baldi family had been handled, settled, put to bed. She was here at the Ricci family's grand New Year's Eve party because they loved to throw lavish parties and loved to include everyone who had helped them. And Charlotte had helped them, having spent the entire autumn in Florence, working to smooth tensions following intense, negative media attention arising from the family's struggles with power, and issues from succession.

Not all issues were completely settled, but much of the tension was gone, and the family had come together to present a unified face to the public once again. Tonight's party was part of that unified face.

She shouldn't have come tonight. Her part was done. She'd been paid—well paid, too. There was no justifiable reason to have returned to Florence for a party.

The music changed, slowed, and Brando pulled her closer, his hand settling low on her back, her breasts crushed to his tuxedo-covered chest. "You're overthinking," he murmured, his breath warm against her ear.

"I am," she agreed. "Or perhaps I should say, I'm thinking. And I should be thinking. You are dangerous."

"I would never hurt you. That is a promise."

And she knew that. She knew he'd be amazing—in bed, out of bed. The chemistry between them was electric and had been there from the moment they'd met last September. But the chemistry is what also troubled her, because she'd never felt a pull like this… She'd never even considered throwing caution to the wind. And yet here she was, a half hour from midnight, wrestling with her conscience, wrestling with desire.

"I shouldn't be here," she whispered, fingers curling around his, her heart thumping too hard, her body warm, sensitive, exquisitely aware…aroused. She hadn't made love in over a year…perhaps two years… She hadn't felt this attracted to anyone… ever. Part of her was so tempted to give in to the heat, while the logical, disciplined part warned that it was a mistake, a mistake that could jeopardize her career, her reputation…

Her heart.

She looked up into his handsome face again. He was gorgeous…truly handsome, but it wasn't just beautiful bone structure. He was smart, fascinating, compelling. During the months of working with the Ricci family, Brando was the one who drew her, time and again. Even though he was the youngest in his family, he had the most wisdom and insight, and she'd come to trust and respect his point of view, even going to him when Enzo, Marcello and Livia couldn't agree on anything, hoping Brando could find a diplomatic way to bring his fractious siblings together. And he had. And he did.

She'd returned tonight to Florence for him.

For this…

Whatever this was.

"What are you afraid of?" he asked now, his narrowed gaze sweeping her face.

His scrutiny made her face tingle, setting countless nerve endings alight. "Losing my head. Losing control."

The corner of his mouth lifted ever so slightly. His hand slid lower on her back, nearly cupping the curve of her butt. "We're two consenting adults."

She could feel his sinewy strength pressed against the length of her. His hard chest, his waist, the powerful thighs. "Yes, but business and pleasure should always be kept separate—"

"We're no longer working together," he reminded, his head dropping, his lips brushing the side of her neck.

She shuddered, and closed her eyes, trying to ignore how her breasts tightened, nipples pebbling, desire coiling within her. It was becoming increasingly difficult to keep a clear head. All she wanted was his mouth on hers, his hands teasing, exploring the length of her. It had been so long since she'd been with anyone and yet she wanted him…wanted his weight on her, wanted his body filling hers, wanted the pleasure she knew he'd give. The pleasure she craved…not from just anyone, but him. Brando Ricci. Vintner. Entrepreneur. Billionaire.

Lover.

No, not her lover, not yet.

"We shouldn't do this," she whispered, air catching in her throat as his thumb stroked the side of her neck, lighting little tongues of fires just beneath the surface of her skin.

"We've done nothing wrong," he murmured. "We're simply dancing."

Done nothing wrong yet, she silently corrected, with *yet* being the operative word.

Charlotte tipped her head back to look up into Brando's mesmerizing silver eyes that were anything but cool, or cold. The heat in them scorched her now and she felt a shiver race through her. She'd fought this attraction for months, fought the sizzling awareness, suppressed the hunger, but tonight she was losing the battle. Just being in his arms was making her breathless and dizzy. Her body hummed, aching with awareness. Hunger.

"It's nearly midnight," she said, glancing over his shoulder at the enormous clock that had been mounted on the wall of the palace ballroom for tonight's New Year's countdown.

He glanced at the clock, too. "Ten minutes."

Her gaze took in the orchestra on the stage playing everyone's favorites, and the throng of beautiful people filling the dance floor. The seventeenth-century ballroom was packed with some of Europe's most glamorous, wealthy people. They were having a wonderful time, laughing, dancing, drinking, celebrating. When the clock struck midnight, the celebration would become deafening.

She'd always hated crowds, and normally avoided

parties, but when the invitation came to attend the Riccis' party, she didn't say no. She couldn't say no.

"What are you thinking, *cara*?" Brando's deep voice was a caress.

Cara, darling. She felt another helpless shiver race through her.

She'd come tonight for him.

She wanted only him.

And yet, her rules. Her stupid rules.

She dampened her lips with the tip of her tongue. "I don't mix—"

"Business and pleasure," he completed for her. "I know. But tonight is not business. We're done with business, done with the family, done doing what others want us to do."

His lips brushed hers, a fleeting kiss that felt as if he'd set a thousand butterflies free inside her heart and mind. Wings of hope. Flutters of possibilities.

She always lived so alone, so controlled, so contained, but tonight… Tonight she felt as if maybe, just maybe, she belonged somewhere, to someone. Even if it were for one night only.

"Just tonight," she said hoarsely. "You must agree this is just one night, and nothing more than that. Promise me, Brando."

His lips brushed hers again. "Fine. Tonight is ours. Tonight belongs to us."

"And tomorrow—"

"We won't worry about. It's not here."

CHAPTER ONE

CHARLOTTE PARKS TUCKED her long pale hair behind an ear, straightened the lapel on her fashionable coat and rang the doorbell on the tall, handsome seventeenth-century building in the heart of Florence, just steps from Ponte Vecchio. Originally constructed as a palace, the building had been turned into several private homes, including the town house for Italian tycoon Brando Ricci.

She'd been here twice before, once for business last October, and once for—well, *not* business—New Year's Eve. It was a large, lavish town house with three separate floors and the sheer size of it meant that it'd take a moment for someone to come to the door, and so she waited calmly, expression serene.

Charlotte was skilled at serene. She'd mastered stress and pressure, having learned how to adjust to instability and conflict early in life, as the next to youngest in a big, rather famous British family, her affluent, aristocratic parents marrying and divorcing with rather joyous abandon, giving her a dozen siblings, half siblings and stepsiblings. She'd been born in England, then hauled to Los Angeles for ten years with her mother when she married the roguish film director Heath Hughes, and then bounced back to Europe at fifteen for finishing school in Switzerland.

Charlotte's siblings and stepsiblings were quite famous in their own right—models, actresses, race car drivers, as well as beautiful, envied English socialites. The Parks-Hughes-horpe family even had their own reality TV show for a bit, before certain members of the family decried it as too common, too crass, too American. It didn't help that nearly half of the family was now American, and full of plans and ambition. Charlotte, having spent twelve years in America, the ten with her mom, and now the past two on her own with a lovely house in the Hollywood Hills, had come to appreciate American bluntness and the efficiency with which Americans tackled problems. Well, maybe that was overstating things. Affluent Americans, inevitably image conscious, were very good at hiring help for damage control, and Charlotte was very good at damage control, so good, she had her own little company that had become a very successful PR company with global clientele.

Her ability to solve problems is what brought her to Florence. She'd met Brando Ricci nine months ago when she was hired to sort out a public relations nightmare involving the legendary Ricci family, one of Italy's most famous families, known for their wine, their leather goods, as well as their modern fashion house.

The Ricci family business dated back to the turn of the century, when making a great Chianti was their claim to fame. Following World War II, the family expanded, adding fashion and luxury leather goods to their business. The three Ricci brothers, grandsons to the founder, grew and nurtured the business until they ran into a rather common problem—how would succession work in a family where the three brothers had been almost equals, and yet each brother had two or three children each? It was one thing to share leadership among three, but a corporation couldn't have eight leaders. She'd stepped in late last August to smooth over some of the negative publicity stemming from the internal family struggles, generating new media coverage that focused on the family's cohesiveness, but behind the scenes, the family was still rather fractious as succession hadn't yet been truly addressed. But she'd done her part. The Ricci family was out of the tabloids, and she'd been given a very generous payment for services, and that should have been that.

Except it wasn't.

Charlotte, who rarely made mistakes, made a critical tactical error on New Year's Eve. She shouldn't have spent a night with Brando Ricci. Yes, it had been an extraordinary night, but letting down one's guard, and breaking one's rules, had staggering consequences.

Now she was here, but she dreaded the moment she'd be face-to-face with him. Brando was brilliant, powerful, perceptive, exciting. He'd made her feel all kinds of things she'd never felt before, and that was while still on the dance floor.

Returning here, being carried up to his bedroom, had been earth-shattering. She wasn't a virgin but she'd never felt anything as exquisite as what she felt in his arms, in his bed. It was without a doubt the most amazing night of her life. The sex had been so good, so unbelievably good, that she'd flown home dazed and dazzled and completely swept away.

Thank goodness there was a huge distance between them—6,188 miles to be precise—a trip that required at least one or two stops, depending on the airline and route, so it wasn't easy, or convenient to jet over to say hello. She returned home determined to focus on the future, not the past, or the bliss of being with a man who knew how to make a woman feel like the most glorious thing in the world.

There would be no reunions, no weekend escapes. They'd had their fling, and yes, it'd been the most exciting, sensual thing she'd ever experienced, but she wasn't going to lose her head over incredible sex with the sexiest, most sensual, most overwhelming man she'd ever met. That would be plain foolish, and she might be slightly, *slightly*, secretly besotted with Brando, but she was no fool. He was completely out of her league, and she'd told him so when he'd phoned to say he'd be in Los Angeles and hoped they could get together.

Just hearing his voice on the phone slammed her back to the night she'd spent in his bed in Florence. She felt his heat and strength again, and could picture his head between her thighs, his mouth on her where she was oh, so sensitive, his tongue finding every delicate nerve so that when she came, she came hard, and completely fell apart, dissolving into tears because he made her feel, so very much, and it was actually too much. She might live in California now but underneath she was still quite British and didn't enjoy being flooded with quite so much emotion. Emotion was wonderful in tidy bites and measured doses, but the emotion Brando made her feel, well… Really, there was no place for it, and no room in her life for dazed, dazzled and befuddled.

Which brought her to this exact moment, where she waited on Brando's doorstep, her elegant swing coat hiding her secret, a secret she had to share, because there was no hiding it any longer. It was one thing to keep a secret when there was no physical evidence, but her bump was impossible to hide now, so here she was, steeling herself for a conversation she did not think she'd ever have. Because she'd been on the pill, and he'd used a condom, and yet…

And yet…

Charlotte's heart staggered and she exhaled hard,

before drawing in a slower calming breath and ringing the doorbell again, pressing on the bell a little longer, and more insistently, than before.

The last time she was here Brando had almost made her believe in miracles. But there were no miracles, just bruised principles, and broken rules, and heart-wrenching consequences.

The front door suddenly swung open, revealing a tall slender young woman with long, dark tousled hair, red lips, her naked body barely covered by a white silk robe, the fabric so sheer, her dusky nipples shone through.

Charlotte recognized the model immediately. She was an Argentinean beauty taking the fashion world by storm.

"Si?" Louisa drawled as her robe slid off her shoulder and down her slender arm, fabric no longer covering one jutting breast.

Charlotte ignored the nipple. *"Brando è disponibile?"* she asked, utilizing the Italian she'd learned at her Swiss finishing school.

Louisa looked her up and down, a sly smile curving her full lips. *"È un po legato."*

He's a little tied up, Louisa had said, and from the model's smug smile, Charlotte had a feeling the words were literal.

"Would you be so kind as to untie him?" she said politely in Italian. "Let him know Charlotte Parks is here. I'll be waiting for him in the grand salon," she added, stepping into the house and heading for the formal room halfway down the white marble hall.

Charlotte heard the door close hard, and then footsteps on the curving staircase that led to the second floor. Brando's bedroom was up there. Charlotte knew, because she'd been there, during that second visit to this house when he'd stripped her naked and turned her into a mass of quivering need. She'd been far too intrigued by him, and she'd been far too confident in her ability to manage him, just the way she managed everything else in the world. But one didn't easily manage Brando Ricci. He was a force to be reckoned with.

That force, all six foot two inches of him, entered the salon, dressed, thankfully, and looking casually handsome in faded denims that wrapped his muscular thighs, and a silver-gray cashmere V-neck sweater that hugged the hard planes of his chest. The cashmere sweater perfectly matched the color of his silver-gray eyes and paired a little too well with the espresso black of his hair.

He was tall, lean, honed and even more beautiful than she remembered. Her heart jumped, a quick staccato that did nothing for her sense of calm. Just that little glimpse of skin at his throat made her remember what it had felt like to be naked against him. His body didn't just look magnificent, he knew how to move it, and when he'd been inside her, she'd felt satisfied, more satisfied, more…everything… than she'd ever felt in her life.

Being intimate with him hadn't been just physical pleasure. She'd experienced a feeling of peace and wholeness, which made no sense since Brando had a history of breaking hearts. He didn't do long relationships. He didn't want commitments.

Which was why he should be fine with her proposal, relieved to hear that she would handle everything.

"Charlotte," he said, approaching her, and leaning down to kiss each of her cheeks. "What brings you to Florence?"

"You do." She smiled up at him. "I hope I haven't interrupted anything."

He gave her an amused smile, indicating he was aware that she was aware she'd obviously interrupted something.

"Shall we sit?" he suggested, gesturing to the chic armchairs in the white room with red and coral accents.

"Yes, thank you." She took the chair opposite his, the chairs a little closer together than she preferred, but it felt good to be off her feet as her heart had begun to race and all her cool, calm confidence deserted her now that he was here. Brando was larger than life, humming with an energy that she found potent and strangely addictive. Her family was filled with beautiful people, but Brando exuded a physicality and a virility that was all his own.

He'd more than impressed her with his virility six months ago in this very house.

New Year's Eve. What a life-changing night…

Heat rushed through her at the memory, and her stomach did a wobbly flip. The last thing she wanted to do was relive those intense memories now, here, with Brando within arm's length and his lover upstairs waiting for him in bed. "I imagine Louisa must be growing impatient," she said.

He smiled, a lazy, almost indulgent smile. "Louisa is good at entertaining herself." He was still smiling, but his silver gaze narrowed, expression sharpening. "When did you arrive in Italy?"

"Today actually. I've left my bags at the hotel, but haven't yet checked in."

"That eager to see me?"

"I wasn't sure if you'd be here, or at the country house. If you were in the countryside already, I was going to rent a car and drive out to meet you."

"I'm heading to the villa tomorrow." His gaze skimmed over her, studying her intently. "You look well."

"Thank you. I feel well." She hesitated, struggling for words, her carefully rehearsed speech forgotten. She'd convinced herself that he wouldn't care about her news. She'd convinced herself that he'd be relieved she was going to handle everything and do everything. Suddenly she wasn't so sure and her heart had begun to race, anxiety pulsing just below the surface. "Do you mind if I take off my coat? It's very warm."

"Yes, your cheeks are quite flushed."

The moment her coat came off, he'd see. He'd know. She hesitated, hands no longer steady, her confidence shaken.

What if it didn't play out the way she anticipated? What if he—

She stopped herself there, unable to imagine any other scenario than the one she'd planned on. He was a bachelor. A playboy. He wasn't father material. He wouldn't be interested in the domestic details.

"Charlotte, are you all right?" he asked.

Tell him. Just tell him now.

Instead, mouth dry, heart racing, she slowly, carefully eased her arms from the sleeves and then allowed the coat to slide off her shoulders and fall back onto the chair.

Her emerald dress was slim fitting, the soft knit clinging to her small frame, highlighting her bump. The baby gave a hard kick just then and she touched her bump, not sure if she was soothing the baby, or herself.

"I'm six months," she said quietly, steadily. "It's been an easy pregnancy, and there have been no complications. I didn't want to say anything until I'd made it out of the first trimester—" She broke off, took a quick breath and plunged on. "I wasn't showing until recently and then I just popped. I couldn't hide it any longer, and I didn't think I should."

"Should I be offering my congratulations?"

"If you'd like to include yourself in the congratulations."

There was a beat of silence. “Is this your way of saying it’s mine?”

“Yes.”

“And you’re sure it’s mine?”

“Yes.”

His gaze held hers, the silver gray piercing. There was no judgment in his eyes, no censure, no shock, not even disappointment. “We took precautions, both of us.”

“It seems we have a child that very much wants to be part of the world,” she answered, sitting tall, shoulders straight.

“A child with determination,” he replied.

She smiled, her most charming smile, aware that they were now both playing the same game. “It’s an admirable trait.”

“Agreed.” He hesitated. “You never considered an abortion?”

“No.” She eyed him cautiously. “Would you have preferred me to end the pregnancy?”

“I’m Italian. Catholic. So, no.”

“I’m neither, but it was never an option.”

His gaze held hers. “And now you’re here.”

“Yes.” Her chin lifted, and yet she kept her voice even. As long as she maintained control, she’d be fine, and he’d be fine. Really, it was just a matter of needing time to work through the shock that he must be feeling. “It seemed best to tell you in person. I knew you would want to know, and you deserve to know. It didn't seem fair to just make all the decisions without consulting you."

Brando arched a brow. "And yet you haven't consulted me."

"I am now. That's why I've come."

Silence stretched and the silence made her pulse do an odd, uncomfortable thudding in her veins, a thudding she felt all the way through her. This was not the Brando she'd last seen. In fact, this was not a Brando she recognized. They were like strangers, and yet the last time she'd been with him they'd been incredibly intimate. She'd given herself all of him and had never regretted it…not until she discovered there were consequences for that night of passion.

"The pregnancy stunned me," she said after a moment. "It wasn't part of my plan, and it took me a few weeks to sort through all my feelings, but I'm actually now very much looking forward to motherhood."

"This consultation… What is your goal? You want money? Financial support?"

"No."

"What, then?"

Her plan was to offer him exactly what he didn't want—a chance to be a father. She'd give him the opportunity to co-parent, an opportunity she knew he wouldn't want, and when he balked, she'd gently offer to do it all herself, and he'd be relieved, and accept. Brando was handsome and brilliant but not ready to settle down. His sister had said so more than once. Brando was the least committed to family. Brando was the rebel and valued his independence. She understood that, though. Charlotte valued hers.

"I want you to be this child's father," she said quietly, "*if* you want to be his or her father, and if not, I am sure one day I will fall in love and marry a man who will raise this child as his. In the meantime, I recognize your rights, and I respect your rights, and would like to include you in the decision making, should you want to be included."

"You were pregnant when I was in Los Angeles earlier in the year."

"Yes."

"Why didn't you tell me then?"

"It was early in my pregnancy, and I wasn't sure that the pregnancy was viable. My sisters have miscarried in the first trimester, and they warned me that it could happen to me."

"Your family knows, then?"

"No. I've managed to hide the pregnancy so far, but it's impossible now. I'm obviously expecting."

"Why haven't you told your family?"

"It's none of their business." She put a hand to her bump again, feeling another fluttery shift inside. "And if I was going to share the news with anyone, it should be you."

Charlotte Parks was every bit as beautiful as the last time Brando had seen her, naked in his bed, her long golden hair splayed across the pillow, her mouth swollen from his kisses. This morning she looked impossibly self-contained, as well as impossibly glowing. Pregnancy suited her. Her skin appeared more luminous, her eyes bluer, brighter, her long, golden blond hair shimmering in the sunlight that poured through the tall windows.

When Louisa had come upstairs to tell him there was a woman at the door, demanding to see him, he'd arched a brow, but hadn't been concerned. When he discovered it was Charlotte in the salon, he'd been intrigued. Charlotte, fascinating Charlotte, never made demands, and yet she'd been pure pleasure in his bed. But now he wasn't as sanguine. Apparently, she was pregnant. With his child.

He'd heard this before, years ago. Thankfully he'd asked for a paternity test, and the test had turned out negative. He couldn't have been more grateful.

Now… Now he didn't know what to think and Brando's gaze swept over Charlotte, skimming her fair hair, high elegant cheekbones, before dropping to her full breasts and her taut, round bump. She looked radiant, but not quite as serene as he'd first thought her to be. "Hasn't this been a difficult secret to keep?" he asked.

"No."

"Really?"

She shrugged. "I'm not one that needs to discuss things to make decisions, and I've never turned to others for advice. What I needed was time, and I had that time, which is why I'm here, ready to discuss the future."

"And yet this is all news to me."

Color swept her lovely high cheekbones, and her head dipped. "True." Her chin lifted and her gaze met his. "I expect you'll want a paternity test. I've already checked into clinics that do the testing here in Florence. It's a simple procedure, just a blood draw for both of us and then we wait for results." She hesitated a moment. "If possible, I'd like to get it done today. That way we'll have the results sooner than later."

"And if I am the father?"

"Well, you are the father, but please let me reassure you that I have things well in control. I'm not asking for anything from you. In fact, nothing in your world needs to change. I just wanted to be courteous—"

He laughed, a low husky sound that stopped her midsentence.

She glanced at him, winged eyebrows arching higher, her color even more heightened. "I wasn't trying to be funny," she said rather stiffly.

"Maybe not, but I found it comical when you said nothing in my world needs to change. *Bella*, everything in my world will change. It's already changed, if I'm to become a father."

"I'm obviously going to become a mother. But you… You don't have to do this…or be part of this. I'm quite comfortable parenting on my own."

"Which would be fine, if it wasn't my child, but if it is my child, then I'm going to be involved."

Her lips parted and then pressed together. She glanced to the tall windows framed by large red-and-white-check silk curtains, the checked fabric a contrast to the marble terra-cotta parquet floor. She suddenly looked anxious and appeared to be struggling to find the right words.

"I'm surprised you're taking this so well," she said at last, looking over at him, her blue gaze clear. "We had one night together, little more than a fling, and yet you seem ready to embrace parenthood."

"I've always taken precautions to prevent an unplanned pregnancy, and yet now that we're here at this crossroads, it's not a tragedy, not something that needs to be overcome. We're mature and independent, able to provide a safe, happy home for our child."

Again, her lips parted, and again they pinched closed. Color washed through her cheeks, her eyes shone overly bright.

It struck him then that he'd caught her off guard. What had she imagined he'd say? No thank you, and goodbye?

That he'd wash his hands of his child?

"But maybe it's not mine," he said, thinking back to that other time where a woman had tried to trick him.

"No, it's yours. Without a doubt. But I didn't expect you to believe me. Why should you? We spent only one night together. Which is why I want the blood test done today. I'm only here for the weekend, and then Monday I head to England for a week, but we should get the results in seven business days, or three, if we pay to rush the results." She drew a breath. "I'd prefer to pay the rush fee, so I could return here and draw up custodial paperwork before my flight back to California."

"Custodial paperwork?" he echoed, thinking she'd certainly mapped it all out.

"The baby will live with me."

Her calm, crisp answer stirred his temper. "It seems we do have things to discuss."

"I just want to reassure you, Brando, that I have no intention of sharing the baby's paternity with anyone. This isn't anyone's business but ours, and the secret will be safe with me."

He lifted a brow. "Our child isn't to know I'm his or her father?"

"Do you want to be a father?" she asked bluntly.

"I don't understand the question, *cara*. If I'm the father, I am the father."

Fresh color swept through her face. "I suppose that is the part we need to discuss."

Was she seriously wanting to cut him out? Was she envisioning him as a sperm donor, but nothing more? He felt a surge of temper, but swiftly checked it. "It seems you and I do have a great deal to discuss," he said, "but I'd prefer more privacy. Now isn't the ideal time, not with Louisa here."

Charlotte glanced up to the ceiling, as if she expected Louisa to be there, on the hand-blown glass chandelier. "True." She slipped her coat back on, opened her handbag and drew out a slip of paper. "This is the nearest clinic that can do the blood draw. They can get you in this afternoon. I'll be going straight there when I leave here. If you could just call and make an appointment for today? Would that be possible?"

"I see no reason for us to delay the test."

"Good, thank you." She rose and tucked her purse beneath her arm. "And I apologize for barging in on you like this. I should have realized you might have a guest."

"It's fine. This was important." He couldn't imagine anything being more important, nor could he imagine any woman more beautiful than Charlotte Parks. He'd wanted her from the very first meeting. She'd been the elusive one, but he hadn't given up…not until she'd returned to Los Angeles and ghosted him.

He walked her to the front door now. "Where are you staying?"

She gave him the name of her hotel, a five-star property overlooking the river. It's where she had stayed before. There were smaller hotels, more affordable hotels, but this one took such excellent care of her the last time she was in Florence, it's where she wanted to be this time.

"Let me call a taxi for you," he said.

"I think I'll walk." She forced a faint smile. "The

fresh air will do me good and maybe then I can get some work done."

"You're still working?"

"But of course." She flashed a smile. "It's what I do best."

"It's not too much at this stage of your pregnancy? It won't hurt the baby?"

"No. Everything is good."

The baby, Charlotte silently repeated as she walked back to her hotel. He'd referenced the baby in such a way that emotion fluttered in her, little wings of pain and heartache.

It was strange talking about her pregnancy. She'd kept the news to herself all this time, carrying the secret within her, just as she carried the baby, close to her heart, protective of the world's reaction. And yet in a matter of minutes she'd shared her news, and Brando had knocked away the walls of secrecy and made the news…matter-of-fact.

She paused at the curb, checked for traffic and dashed across, grateful for the brisk walk, needing the quick pace to help her process everything she was thinking and feeling.

All this time she'd thought she was most concerned about the pregnancy, about becoming a single mother, but seeing Brando had stripped away the pretense.

Seeing him made her feel naked and nervous and incredibly vulnerable.

She didn't have feelings for him, and yet…

Charlotte exhaled hard, and blinked even harder, and wondered why she felt so terribly discombobulated. Seeing Brando made her feel…strange.

Raw.

Hurt.

Which didn't make sense as he'd been nothing but polite, and respectful considering how shocking her announcement had to have been. She was grateful there had been no drama and he'd been quite cordial about taking the paternity test. The lack of drama made her suspect, though, striking her as too good to be true.

Maybe Brando was in shock. Maybe he wasn't as sanguine as he appeared, and underneath his veneer of calm, he was secretly rattled.

Or maybe he didn't believe her and was just waiting for the test results before challenging her…

Or maybe he wasn't even thinking about her news anymore and maybe he was back in bed with Louisa.

She blanched, and her stomach rose.

Oh, why, oh, why did Louisa have to be there today? And why, oh, why did Charlotte have to know about her?

Brando left the clinic across the street from Maria Beatrice Hospital and called Charlotte. It took her a few rings to answer the phone.

"It's Brando," he said when she answered. "Am I interrupting anything?"

"No. Just trying to write a press release but can't focus. I didn't sleep well last night."

"You should try to nap."

"Maybe," she said.

"What are you doing later?" he asked. "Do you have plans for dinner tonight?"

"No. Just more work."

"Have dinner with me."

"Did you have the test done?"

"I did, and we should have results in the morning. There is a lab here in Florence that will expedite testing for us."

"How? I heard three days was the fastest—"

"Unless you pay enormous sums of money to get something done."

"Ah."

He heard the wary note enter in her voice. "So, dinner?"

"What about Louisa?"

"She's not invited."

"Brando."

"Can we just focus on you for the time being? You're here, six months pregnant. Isn't it time we finally started communicating?"

CHAPTER TWO

BRANDO WATCHED CHARLOTTE emerge from the hotel's elevators and cross the marble lobby. Unlike this morning's form-fitting dress that had outlined her shape, she had chosen narrow black trousers and a stylish white tunic that skimmed her stomach, the tunic's natural fullness making the bump harder to detect.

Suddenly he flashed back to a different pregnancy with a different woman. It was years ago and when confronted by the news of her pregnancy, he'd been horrified. They'd had a brief relationship, and it had ended when he discovered she was not at all what she seemed, her vivacious, sparkling beauty a cover for an insecure, unkind, manipulative personality. It filled him with dread to think of her raising any child of his, and yet he'd promised her he'd support her and the baby...if the baby truly was his.

Thank God, the blood test came back negative. The child wasn't his. Adele had cried and protested, claiming the DNA blood test flawed.

It was only much later that he'd learned she'd manipulated some other wealthy man to marry her.

The pregnancy scare had been a wake-up call, and for a while Brando didn't date, choosing to be celibate over risking paternity claims. But after an eight-month celibacy period, he began dating again, and now here he was, waiting for the results of another DNA test.

He didn't like comparing Adele to Charlotte, though. They were nothing alike, and to be honest, Brando didn't need a paternity test to prove he was the father of Charlotte's baby. She wouldn't have come here, to him, if she hadn't been certain. Charlotte had money of her own, as well as a successful career. She'd even said earlier that she wanted nothing from him, and was planning on raising the baby in California, apart from him.

Which would be fine if it was someone else's child, but if the baby was his, since the baby was his, Brando was not going to be forced to the sidelines.

He'd taken the paternity test this afternoon to fight for his rights. He was going to be part of his child's life, and not as a distant figure on the periphery, but as a hands-on parent who was present from birth.

He moved toward Charlotte now, meeting her near the reception desk. "You look lovely," he said, greeting her with a kiss on the cheek.

She stiffened at the kiss, shooting him a suspicious look. "No need for compliments. This isn't a date."

"Would you prefer I had said something along the lines that you're very punctual?" he replied mockingly.

"Yes."

"Charlotte, good to see you. You're very punctual tonight."

She shot him another disapproving glance. "It's discourteous making people wait."

"You must have hated it when Marcello showed up an hour late for our first meeting."

"I wasn't impressed, no." And then her expression softened a fraction. "But you were on time. You're always on time."

"Speaking of time, we have a reservation in ten minutes. We can drive there, or walk, if you're feeling up to it. The restaurant isn't far." He glanced down at her feet. She was wearing pumps with a stylish kitten heel. "Would you prefer to drive, or walk?"

"I'd love to walk."

"Good. I was hoping you'd say that." Brando placed his hand lightly on her lower back and steered her out the front door, where he handed the keys of his car to the hotel valet.

Charlotte was exquisitely aware of Brando's hand on the small of her back as they left the hotel. He'd smelled heavenly when he'd kissed her in the lobby.

It had been just a brief kiss on the cheek, and yet the warm brush of his lips and the light spicy scent he wore made her stomach curl and breath catch. He was sin on two legs, and her undoing.

"Where are we going for dinner?" she asked, trying to distract herself.

He named a restaurant she wasn't familiar with and for a few minutes they made small talk about Florence's cuisine. It was an inane conversation, she thought, as superficial as it could be, but also better than talking about what was really at stake.

The baby, and the future.

"You really think they will have results from the blood test tomorrow?" she asked, glancing from the golden sky to Brando.

"They said they might be able to rush something tonight, but we'd know for sure in the morning."

Charlotte wasn't worried he wasn't the father. He was the only one she'd been with in years, but she didn't expect him to take her word for it. After all, she'd slept with him on the first date. Why should he not think she did that all the time?

"Are you nervous?" he asked.

Her brow furrowed. "About the results? No. I think I'm more overwhelmed just seeing you again. It's…surreal."

"You had no plans to see me again, did you?"

She glanced up at him again, her gaze skimming his handsome profile. "No," she answered honestly. "I didn't. I don't mix business and pleasure, and once I'd slept with you, I wasn't going to be able to see you, or work with you, again."

"Why did you sleep with me, then?"

She mustered a small, tight smile. "I think you know the answer to that."

"If I did, I wouldn't have asked."

"I found you quite irresistible," she said, her voice lightly mocking. "And I thought, why not, just once, live a little? I should have remembered there are always consequences—" She broke off, stumbling, her toe catching in one of the cobbled stones lining the street. She didn't fall, though. Brando's arm tightened around her, keeping her upright.

"I've got you," he said.

He certainly did. His arm felt like a hot brand around her waist, his fingers sending forks of lightning through her middle. He was so very close and she felt completely overwhelmed by his nearness, creating an aching awareness she didn't want or need. Brando was already her kryptonite. If she wasn't very careful, she'd implode.

"Maybe," she said carefully, as she stopped walking, "I would be steadier without you."

"I don't want you to trip."

"I'm klutzy because you are close. I'd feel surer of myself if you didn't touch me." She tried to keep her tone light. "It must be a pregnancy thing where my center of balance is changing."

He looked skeptical, his silver gaze penetrating. "I was barely touching you."

Heat rushed through her, his words reminding her of the night where he did touch her, all over, giving her endless pleasure. She'd never felt anything like that, and doubted she'd ever feel anything like that again. He'd taken sex and elevated it to an art form. Making love with him had been transcendental…transformative.

"Nonetheless, I find it unsettling." The words sounded harsh, and so she added, "Take that as a compliment if you can. I might be six months pregnant, but you're still you, and apparently, I can't help responding to you."

Brando faced her on the street. "What we had was good, wasn't it?"

"Too good. I didn't trust it." She realized they were blocking the sidewalk and people were having to walk around them, some glancing at Brando and nodding, recognizing him. "We should keep walking."

Five minutes later they arrived at a building tucked off a hidden street not far from one of the famous squares. They took stairs down into the cellar. The walls were frescoed, the floor covered in thick tiles, the beams of the ceiling stenciled in shades of blue, red and gold. There were perhaps a dozen tables, almost all booths framed by rich burgundy velvet curtains. Italian glass chandeliers hung over each table, creating a mosaic of glittering light within each cozy booth.

They were seated at a table in the far corner

away from the other guests. No one had paid them any attention when they arrived and Charlotte was happy to be off her feet, tucked into their booth, the cushion covered in rich, midnight-blue brocade with hints of gold thread, and yet her pulse raced and butterflies filled her. She couldn't remember when she'd last felt so worried. She hadn't been nervous when she'd arrived in Florence this morning, but ever since leaving Brando's house, she'd struggled. "I didn't think this would be easy," she said bluntly, "but at the same time, I didn't think it would be quite so difficult."

"Have I been difficult?"

"No. You haven't. But at the same time, I'm rattled."

"What is troubling you?"

She didn't know how to put her worries into words. She didn't know how to explain her feelings. They weren't making sense to her. How could they make sense to him?

She hadn't come to Italy expecting a declaration of love from Brando. She hadn't come imagining that he would even want to be part of her future. They'd had a one-night stand, and that was really all it was, and she'd had realistic expectations about what he'd say and do. And yet for some reason, seeing Louisa at the front door in that sheer negligee had maddened a small part of her brain, torturing her with a jealousy she couldn't, *shouldn't*, feel. There was no relationship between her and Brando, and certainly no commitment, or feelings of any kind, so why should remembering Louisa make her feel heartsick, and anxious, and angry?

And why should remembering Brando appearing in the salon, handsome and sophisticated and oh, so very calm, make Charlotte feel almost impotent with need, and pain?

That was the part that baffled her.

Why had she been so upset today?

Why did she feel cheated?

How could she possibly feel resentful, and played, when Brando wasn't even hers?

"I can't read your mind, *cara*. You'll have to try to use words," he said.

"It's ridiculous. You'll think I'm ridiculous—"

"I won't."

"No," she corrected, "you will, because I find myself ridiculous right now." She fiddled with the trio of stemware on the table, adjusting the glasses, forming them into a line. "I'm usually incredibly confident, and yet I've been rattled by your girlfriend Louisa." Charlotte glanced at Brando and shrugged. "I'm sorry. It sounds petty—"

"No, it doesn't. You're pregnant and feeling quite alone—"

"I wouldn't go that far. I'm excited about the baby. But seeing Louisa at your door made me realize how weird this really is. I should have called you first. I shouldn't have just shown up."

"It's fine."

"Louisa must be upset."

"She doesn't know. I haven't said anything to her."

"That makes sense, especially as you need to wait for results from the DNA test."

"I'm certain the results will show I'm the father."

She nodded. "They will." She hesitated. "And then you'll tell her?"

"No one needs to know anything, not right now."

She sighed with relief and felt some of her tension knotting her shoulders ease. "Thank you. I'm not ready for the world to know."

"I agree."

Charlotte then had another troubling thought. "But Brando, if you keep the information from her, it's going to cause trouble, it has to."

"Louisa and I are having fun. It's not a serious relationship."

"Do you ever have serious relationships?"

He cocked an eyebrow. "Do you really want to discuss my relationship history tonight?"

Charlotte grimaced. "No. I'm quite sure that's more than I could handle."

Brando laughed softly, the sound low and husky. "Before we put the subject of Louisa behind us, let me just reiterate that Louisa is lovely and fun, but we're not serious, or exclusive.

"You and me being here, having dinner together, isn't problematic, nor is it deceptive. We're not going behind Louisa's back. She knows I'm out with you tonight, just as I know she's with others tonight. So, you don't need to worry about her, or fear that you're stepping on toes."

"And yet she opened your front door almost naked."

"She's a bit of an exhibitionist. She enjoys the attention. Don't let her overly upset you. You've come a long way to meet with me and address the issue of co-parenting—"

"Co-parenting? Is that what you're thinking?"

"I'm the father."

Charlotte's chest squeezed. Her pulse began to race. Panic set in. "What if you're not?"

He gave her a look that made her stomach somersault.

"You are," she said lowly, "but I didn't think… didn't assume…" She couldn't finish the thought. She felt sick. Her limbs felt cold. She struggled to find her center and breathe. *Keep calm, keep calm, keep calm.* "You're a bachelor, living the bachelor lifestyle."

"You're single, as well."

"But I'm not dating others, and not sleeping around—" She stared at him horrified, and yet unable to take the words back. "What I mean is, we live really far apart. It's not as if we can fly a baby back and forth across the Atlantic."

He said nothing, but she felt the weight of her words between them as well as the accusation.

He was still sleeping with others. She was upset

that he was sleeping with others. She hadn't even phrased it as nicely as that. She'd made him sound like a tomcat.

She waited for him to speak. And still he kept silent. She went hot and cold, hating to now be on the defensive. "You are a bachelor. You can do whatever you please. I apologize if I sounded critical of your lifestyle."

"Is that why you've waited so long to tell me about the baby?"

"No." She forced herself to meet his silver gaze. "No, I promise. I waited because… I didn't want to share the news."

"Share the news, or share our child?"

It felt as if he'd struck her in the chest. She inhaled hard, pain splintering her heart.

"I live in California."

"And I live here."

She picked through his words, processing the meaning. "Do you truly desire to be part of our child's life?"

"Absolutely. Any child of mine will be raised by me."

Another blow that made her throat thicken and her eyes sting. "By you?"

"My father was a hands-on parent, and I intend to be the same."

"How can you be so sure you want to do this?"

"I would never walk away from my responsibilities." He hesitated. "Would it make you feel better if I offered to be the custodial parent? I'd raise our child—"

"*No.* Not an option."

"Then why is it an option for you to be the sole custodial parent?"

"Because I'm making this baby. I'm carrying it right now."

"And you wouldn't be making a baby if it weren't for my sperm that found a way to reach your egg."

"I don't need the biology lesson, Brando."

"And I will not permit you to cut me out. I might not be carrying our child, but I am as committed to his or her future as you are."

Things had escalated quickly, she thought, dazed. She sat back, stunned, and uncertain as to what to say in response.

The waiter appeared with a bottle of sparkling water and after a few words from Brando, cleared away the wineglasses.

Silence stretched and Charlotte's eyes stung, hot and gritty. Six months ago, she'd had sex with Brando, sex that resulted in three unforgettable orgasms, and one very unplanned pregnancy. "I didn't want any of this to happen," she said quietly. "I've never mixed business with pleasure, never, ever, until you, and now everything is a mess."

"Not that much of a mess," he answered. "We're two capable adults. We will sort things out and come up with a plan that puts the baby's needs first, because in the end, that is the important thing."

It wasn't a question, but a statement. It crossed her mind that she was seriously in over her head, because she'd had a plan, a good plan, but he'd just tossed it out and now they were starting over, and she had a feeling she wasn't going to like the new plan at all.

"There's no reason to rush, though," she said after a length pause. "We should take time to consider all the different options. The baby won't be here for three months, and that gives us time to discuss the pros and cons of each option. The last thing we want to do is let our hearts overrule our heads."

He studied her from across the table, the glittering light captured in his narrowed silver gaze and casting shadows beneath his high, hard cheekbones. Brando was no longer smiling. His jaw was hard, lips pressed firm. "Time will not change what is right. My duty is to my child, and the needs of my child come first now."

"I just thought you might want more time… You've only just learned about the pregnancy today. I worry you're being impulsive—"

"You didn't expect me to assume responsibility?"

"I—" She broke off, glanced away, the tip of her tongue moistening her dry lower lip. "I thought you'd be more ambivalent. I thought there might be more resistance."

"Why, if it's my son or daughter?"

"It took me weeks to get to the place you've reached in hours."

"Sex is how babies are made. I've always been cognizant that sex, as pleasant as it is, leads to procreation."

The waiter returned and there was no menu to read. The waiter rattled off the house specialties and Brando recommended the *bistecca alla Fiorentina*, claiming it was the best Florentine steak in the city.

"I won't be able to eat very much," she answered, "and I'm craving pasta. I thought I heard *crespelle* mentioned. Is that the dish that's similar and stuffed with ricotta cheese and spinach?"

"Yes. It's good here, too."

"I'll just have the *crespelle* and salad."

Brando spoke quickly to the waiter, placing their order. The waiter topped off their water glasses and left them alone.

"You didn't order wine," she said.

"You're not drinking so I won't drink," he said.

"I don't mind if you drink. You're a vintner."

"I'm not giving up wine forever. I just don't need any tonight." He studied her, expression hard. "Did you really think I'd agree to let my child be raised on the other side of the world?"

"I thought you'd react differently, yes."

"What did you expect?"

"That you'd be noncommittal, ask for a pregnancy test and then make me wait while you came to terms with the fact that I'm truly carrying your baby."

"Did you ever think it might possibly be someone else's?"

It was a fair question. It shouldn't put her on edge. She felt defensive, though. "No. You have been the only man I've slept with in the past year."

There was a subtle shift in his expression, his black lashes dropping ever so slightly over his piercing gaze. "Why?"

"I only sleep with someone I'm profoundly attracted to." She lifted her chin, smiled wryly. "I was profoundly attracted to you."

"Surely there are other men who catch your eye."

"Apparently not often enough." She pushed back a long pale strand of hair, tucking it behind her ear. "On the plus side, it made the question of parentage easy. You've been the only one I've slept with this year, so, you're it."

"Yet we used birth control."

"My pill, plus your two condoms." She felt hot bands form across her cheekbones. "Obviously, my pill wasn't effective."

"Nor were the condoms."

"I blame myself," she said. "Not you. It's why I'm on the pill. So there are no oops, no mistakes."

"And yet we still have an oops baby."

Her eyes met his and held. "I'd like to raise the baby at my home in Los Angeles. I have a lovely garden and I'm close to the ocean—"

"I don't live in California, *cara*."

She ignored the endearment as she held her

breath, silently counting to ten. She needed to remain calm. "Perhaps you could buy a place near me. Perhaps you could make Southern California a second home."

"But it's not, nor will it ever be."

"I'll be there, and the baby—"

"Or, I kidnap you, keep you locked up at one of my estates."

She waited for him to smile or laugh. He did neither. "You wouldn't do that."

"You don't think so?"

Her insides did a nervous flip. He was being outrageous and she wasn't worried he'd kidnap her, but she understood the point he was making. He wasn't just going to walk away from them. He was asserting his rights. Brando would be a permanent part of their lives, and that was what made her heart race, and her anxiety spike. Brando wasn't one to be managed. Brando Ricci tended to do the managing. "No, you wouldn't do something illegal," she said lightly, feigning calm. "It would be bad for business, and we both know you're very serious about your family business and protecting your family's reputation."

"But even more protective of my child. If I'd go to great lengths to ensure the safety of the business, imagine what I'd do for my son or daughter."

Her pulse jumped yet again and she felt downright nauseous now. This was not going well. She'd thought she'd been prepared for these conversations, but clearly she'd forgotten Brando's strength and focus. "The point being that you'd never do anything to risk your reputation, and that includes your child's."

"Which is why I should whisk you away to keep you out of the public eye until we've figured out what we're going to do."

"I wish I could say that being whisked away sounded appealing—and yes, it does have a certain *Roman Holiday* sound to it—but I'm only here through the weekend. I fly into London Monday early afternoon."

"So soon?"

"I was actually worried that three days was far too long." She glanced up at the hard planes of his striking face, her gaze briefly meeting his, the silver-gray irises piercing, before looking away. Just that brief look into his eyes made her feel hot and tingly. If she could go back in time and change the past, she would. She would have never given herself to Brando, never allowed herself to imagine that she'd be able to handle all the complications of a night spent with him. "Why did I need to be here for three days? We'd have a conversation, you'd get a blood test and then we'd talk after the results were in. But it's not going like that. We're talking now as if we know the results—"

"Because we do. It's my child."

"But that doesn't mean we have to decide everything tonight. We have months—"

"No. We're not putting this off, and we're not going to try to negotiate with you in California. We're going to come to an agreement now, while you're here, and we get it in writing, and notarized, so that it's legal and binding."

"I'm not a runaway bride, Brando. I'm not going to disappear on you."

"How do I know that?"

"Because I'm giving you my word."

"That's a start."

"You don't believe me?"

"You waited six months to tell me I'm going to be a father."

"As I said this morning, I wanted to be sure the pregnancy was viable."

He said nothing for the longest time, and then, "Are we going to need lawyers? Should we just take it to court—?"

"Why would you say that? We don't need lawyers, and we don't need anyone else telling us how to do this. We're smart and reasonable. Surely we can come up with a plan between us."

"So, you'd be willing to live here?"

"I don't think that's necessary."

"You'd rather a newborn baby spend its first year in the air, flying back and forth between Los Angeles and here? That must be eleven hours or more in the air, without connections."

"No, of course not. That's why I think the first year the baby should be with me."

"And then you hand the baby over to me for a year?" he asked, expression blank.

She shuddered. "*No.* I'm not ever handing my baby over, not to you, not to anyone."

"So, we do need lawyers."

"Don't go straight there. Can't we at least try to talk this out?"

"I think you should live here the first few years. Your work is flexible. Your work isn't tied to a place. Whereas I'm a vintner. I can't abandon the grapes."

"Not all your work is in Chianti. You have other business endeavors—"

"So, let me get this straight. You want me to know about my child, but not be involved. You don't want support, either. You just want me to pretend this child doesn't exist, and let you do whatever it is you want?"

Her stomach cramped. She balled her hand into a fist. "That's not what I'm saying."

"Then how are you including me? Where is the space for me, *cara*?"

She didn't answer the question, but then, how could she? Her answer wouldn't have been positive, or flattering, but at least Brando understood Charlotte's intentions. She was doing the correct thing—informing him of the pregnancy—but then she was shutting him out. She didn't truly want him raising the baby with her. She wanted to be mother and father on her own.

That wasn't an option, but he chose to change the subject to keep her from jumping up and leaving.

He asked about a publicity campaign she'd been part of last winter, and as the subject changed, so did the tension. After a few minutes, he could see her relax. They discussed friends they had in common, as well as what was happening with the Ricci business right now.

Dinner arrived and conversation died as they ate, but at least it wasn't an uncomfortable silence. If anything, Charlotte looked thoughtful. He caught her looking at him several times, her brow furrowed, lips pursed.

"I hope you know that I would have never not told you about the baby," she said quietly after Brando ordered a coffee. "I wouldn't have ever kept his or her existence a secret from you. I'm not duplicitous. I genuinely needed time to wrap my head around the pregnancy, and the ramifications. Being a single parent will take work, but we can make it work."

"Why didn't you ask me to come to you in California?" he returned.

"And what would I have said to lure you there?"

"That you're pregnant. That you need me."

She ducked her head, but he could see the wash of hot pink in her cheeks. "I don't generally need people," she said after a moment. "They need me."

Suddenly he understood her in a way he never had before.

Charlotte wasn't playing games. She wasn't trying to cut him out—not in the way he'd first imagined—but she truly believed she was better off trusting no one, relying on no one, and just taking care of everything herself. It wasn't out of cockiness, or arrogance, but survival. This was how she functioned. This was what had allowed her to be successful.

"People make messes and I clean them up," she added with a faint smile, but the smile didn't reach her eyes. "I'm good at problem-solving. Rather exceptional, if I do say so myself."

"It's why we hired you last summer," he answered. "You were exceptional."

"I still am."

This was why he'd been so drawn to her. She was smart, articulate, gorgeous and passionate. The one night only hadn't been his rule, but hers. He hadn't liked making rules, or liked letting her make the rules, but he'd agreed because he'd wanted her that much.

He still wanted her, but everything was different now. This, between them, was no longer about sex, but family, and commitment. He couldn't think of her as an object of desire, but as the mother of his child.

"You might not like admitting it, but you do need

me, *cara*," he said quietly, "and our child needs me, too. Let me in. Try to trust me a little bit."

"I will try, but it's not easy."

"You said you fly out Monday."

"Yes."

"It's Friday. That gives us the weekend to talk and make plans. Let's go to my house in the country. It will be quiet there, and we can discuss the future undisturbed."

She hesitated. "I don't know if that's a good idea. Being alone together created this situation we're now in."

"I'm not going to seduce you, if that's what you're worried about."

"I don't expect you to, not when there are other women in your life now, but I think we have to be clear in our intentions. Yes, I'm carrying your child, but I'm not yours, and you're not mine, and we don't have a relationship. We've never had a relationship. We had sex."

"Your point being?"

"One night of intimacy doesn't equate a relationship, so it's going to be very difficult for me to imagine a future where we do anything together, but I will try provided you realize that I'm not going to give up who I am, and what I want to do, just to please you."

Charlotte tried not to fidget as they waited for the bill to be brought. Her pasta had been excellent, but her nerves had kept her from eating too much.

Their waiter, who had been attentive during the meal, now seemed to have disappeared, perhaps going on a dinner break of his own. Worse, she and Brando weren't speaking.

They sat at the table looking in opposite directions when he suddenly reached for his phone, tapped the screen and read something.

"The results are in," he said, his tone without emotion. "I am the father."

"There never was doubt at my end," she answered.

"Nor mine." He put away the phone. "But at least we have definitive confirmation, because people will ask."

"You mean, your family will ask."

"Of course they'll be interested."

"Even though it's none of their business?"

"That's where you're wrong, *cara*. It is their business. My child will become part of the business. You of all people, having worked with my family, should know that."

After returning Charlotte to her hotel, Brando drove home, and parked his car in his garage, but couldn't make himself go inside, his thoughts too tangled, his emotions intense, to the point of being overwhelming.

He was going to be a father.

A *father*.

It wasn't a hoax this time, or a game. The paternity test was positive. Charlotte was carrying his baby.

His.

Brando pocketed his car key and walked away from his house, heading toward the Arno, which flowed through historic Florence on its way to the sea. He walked along the riverbank to the medieval Ponte Vecchio with its multitude of shops.

Brando knew Florence intimately. He'd grown up here, not far from this very spot, just as his father had, and his grandfather before him.

Now he'd be a father, and he could raise his child here, too, or maybe in the countryside, maybe at his *castello* in the Chianti Valley.

Either way, his child would know and love Tuscany, just as he loved Tuscany, and the soil and grapes of Tuscany.

It was what it meant to be a Ricci. Passion. Perseverance. Commitment.

CHAPTER THREE

CHARLOTTE SLEPT BADLY, her sleep restless with dreams of Brando. Kissing him, making love with him…fighting with him, hiding from him, dreaming one dream after the other.

And now he was back at her hotel, driving the same classic sports car he'd driven to her hotel last night. It was a sleek glossy black car, a collector's car no doubt, a car that matched his sophisticated style and impossibly handsome face.

"I left the roof up," he said, "but if you prefer, I can put it down."

It was a beautiful early June day, the warm weather hinting at the summer heat to come. There would be no rain, nothing but gorgeous blue sky all day. "Is it too much trouble to put it down?" she asked.

"Not at all. You won't mind all the air?"

"I'd like it. It might help blow the cobwebs out of my brain."

"You didn't sleep well?"

"I'm having a hard time adjusting to the time change. I don't usually. Not sure what's changed," she said lightly.

"I do," he answered, "and I think you do, too. Maybe it's time to stop pretending everything is 'normal.' Nothing is normal. Nothing will ever be quite the same again, either."

She stiffened, even as dread swept through her. What did he mean by that? It sounded so ominous, and yet Brando wasn't negative, or pessimistic. Perhaps she was just overreacting. Perhaps her exhaustion was making her overly prickly. "There will certainly be some changes," she answered, "but nothing problematic. Nothing I can't handle," she added.

"That's a good attitude," he said.

Charlotte fought the urge to scream. She was losing control, wasn't she? It wasn't her imagination. Brando was slowly seizing the upper hand, bit by bit, smile by smile, encouraging word by encouraging word.

She'd come to Florence expecting tension, and drama, especially after the results of the paternity test came in, but Brando was anything but tense, or angry. He wasn't cold or detached. He was kind… calm. Solicitous. He was managing her, versus the other way around, and that would end badly. She knew it'd end badly. She'd seen how he worked, and how he turned situations to his advantage.

She should have had a better plan.

She should have remembered how smart he was. How strategic.

"I was worried about you flying at this stage of your pregnancy," he added, his hand light on her back as he walked to his car, and yet the possession was clear. He was acting as if she was his, and the baby was his. He was acting as if they belonged to him. But they didn't.

She stepped away from him and gave him a pointed look. "No touching," she said under her breath. "Remember?"

"*Cara*, I do this for every little old lady, including my grandmother."

Annoyed, she bit her tongue and gave her head a short, sharp shake.

"I might as well be a cane," he added soothingly.

She wasn't soothed. Her nerve endings tingled. She felt hot all over, hot and incredibly aware of him, as well as aware of the night spent together. It wasn't all that long ago. Just months ago. And it had been the most sensual, memorable night of her life, a night so full of passion and sensation that she didn't think she'd ever be the same.

She certainly didn't think she'd have to be here, now, dealing with him.

She'd allowed herself to do everything because she hadn't thought she'd ever see him again…

"What's wrong?" he asked. "Why are you aggravated?"

"I'm not aggravated. And I'm not a senior citizen, Brando, nor am I in need of assistance. I'm strong, and capable, and really happy not being helped," she answered tersely, hating herself for wishing his hand would return to her lower back, wanting the press of his fingers against the curve of her spine. Her body felt even more sensitive now that she was pregnant, and for some reason her libido was even stronger than before. She dreamed erotic dreams at night. During the day, she found herself wanting more, fantasizing about making love, and since that wasn't an option, she'd pleasured herself once, and the orgasm was so intense she'd worried that she might have hurt the baby, and so she hadn't done that again…even though she still craved touch and sensation. Satisfaction.

Brando opened the car's passenger door, and she settled into the sports car's low seat, feeling decidedly awkward. Her center of balance was changing, and her narrow skirt hindered her movement. Brando waited patiently, though, before closing the door behind her even as the hotel bell captain finished putting her bags in the trunk of the car.

Brando then went to work putting the convertible top down, which required just a couple of adjustments on his part, and then he was done.

"Was the international flight taxing?" he asked, returning to the driver's side and sliding behind the steering wheel.

He was dressed in a pale gray linen shirt and gray linen trousers, the shirt open at his throat, sleeves rolled back on his forearms. His throat and chest were tanned, the same burnished color of his arms. It took effort for her to focus on his words and not his lean, powerful body.

"I flew business here so I had my legs up," she answered, "and that definitely helped. But this is probably my last international trip until the baby arrives."

"Do you know if we're having a boy or girl?" he asked, shifting into Drive and pulling away from the hotel to merge into traffic.

She tensed all over at his use of *we* and she glanced at him, studying his profile as he focused on the congestion ahead caused by a truck delivering sleek modern leather couches to an interior design store. The truck was blocking a lane and drivers were honking. "Does it matter to you if I'm carrying a boy or girl?" she asked.

"No."

She wasn't sure she believed him. "Would you really love a daughter as much as the son?"

"I might love a daughter more," he said with a faint shrug.

She didn't know why but his words made her heart ache. Her father hadn't been unloving, but he hadn't been particularly affectionate, or attentive. She'd always thought if she was a horse he would have loved her more. He adored his horses.

She'd once wanted to be adored. She'd wanted

him to miss her the way he'd missed them when away for too long.

He never did, though, and her mother had never really missed her, either, not even when she'd gone to Switzerland for boarding school.

Charlotte had learned to fill her time, and she'd learned the art of distraction. Don't think too much, don't feel hardly anything. Work, focus, achieve.

Those three things had become her mantra, and her mantra had made her successful.

She could still be successful as a mother. She'd certainly be a more devoted parent than either of her parents. She'd make sure her child knew he or she was loved and wanted.

Finally, Charlotte would have a family of her own. Finally, she'd have someone she could shower with love…

"There are no disadvantages to being a girl." Brando's deep voice drew her attention.

Charlotte glanced at him, heart suddenly too tender. "But there might be with a boy," she said.

He lifted a brow. "How so?"

She adjusted her seat belt around her middle and tried to make herself more comfortable. The interior of the sports car was small and Brando was close, his hand resting on the stick shift just inches from her knees. She could smell whatever he was wearing—aftershave, cologne, body spray. It was light, and sexy and very masculine. Between his heady scent, and the warmth radiating off him, she felt painfully aware of him. "I don't want to quarrel. I'm too tired today to quarrel—"

"Why would we quarrel?"

"Because if I'm carrying a boy, you might feel differently about being…involved. It might influence you somehow."

"How so?"

She swallowed hard. "This isn't the best time. I don't want to do this now—"

"Do what? Discuss the future?"

"Yes."

"But that's why you've come to Florence."

"But you're taking over, dictating everything—"

"You've had six months to be in charge. It's time I had a say, don't you think?"

She gritted her teeth, battling her anger, battling fear. She wasn't just losing control, she'd lost it. She'd been a fool to come to Florence without a proper plan, a fool to think it'd go any other way. For a split second she wished she'd never come to Italy, wished she'd never told him about the pregnancy, but just as quickly as the thought came, she smashed it. It wasn't right, or fair, not to Brando, and not to their child. Their child had a right to a father as much as a mother. "I hate this," she whispered. "I hate all of it."

He said nothing for a long moment, his jaw hard, his eyes narrowed as he concentrated on the road. And then after an interminable silence, he said, "You hate me."

Her eyes burned. It hurt to swallow. “I don’t hate you.” Charlotte blinked back the sting of tears. “I hate that we’re going to be playing tug-of-war with our baby. I hate that he or she will never have what I always dreamed of—a stable, unified, loving family. A family that stays together, sticks together, through thick and thin.”

Silence followed her words. Charlotte knotted her hands in her lap, feeling raw and exhausted. Was it only yesterday she’d arrived in Florence? Was it only yesterday she’d knocked on Brando’s door, feeling confident of her plans?

“It doesn’t have to be acrimonious between us,” Brando said, breaking the silence. “There’s no reason we can’t be unified, and supportive of each other, and when the baby is with me, he or she will have a supportive and stable family. A loving family. The Riccis might argue over succession within the business—”

“Might argue? Brando, you all hired me because your fights were making headline news.”

He shrugged dismissively. “We’re Italian. We’re passionate.”

“It’s more than being passionate. Your family is in the middle of a battle over leadership, and the Riccis don’t separate business from family. You might call yourself the Ricci family, but it’s truly about the Ricci business.”

“Your point being?”

“I don’t want my child to be dragged into that.

I'd hate for our child to become part of that scramble for power and position."

"Any child of mine will automatically become of the Ricci family, and thus the Ricci legacy. Boy or girl, he or she will play a role in the family—"

"Business," she added.

His broad shoulders shifted again. "You're right, in my family, it is one and the same. Family. Business. We're one family working together to succeed."

"Except you all weren't working together. You were at odds with each other—"

"We were, until you came along and helped shift the focus on what we weren't doing right, onto what we were doing right. You helped us focus our vision, our mission and our internal communication." He glanced at her, lips twisting. "We're stronger than we were before, thanks to you."

His words gave small comfort. She put a hand to her taut belly, uneasy, and worried. "Will an American child be welcomed into your very Tuscan, old-world family?"

"You're not American. You're British."

"I like living in America, though. I plan on remaining there, raising the baby there, so yes, the baby will be—"

"No."

She stiffened at his brusqueness, and for a moment there was just silence before she said quietly,

"You like America. You have many American friends, particularly in Napa Valley."

"Yes, I do, but I'll never agree to my child being raised apart from me. That's not even an option."

Her pulse kicked up a notch. "Since we're being honest, tell me. What would you do with a small baby?"

"The same thing you'd do." He glanced at her, features hard. "I'm an uncle to a half-dozen nieces and nephews and we get together a lot. I've been part of their lives since they were born."

"Being an uncle isn't the same thing as being a father. Parenting is full-time work—"

"Which is why we should do it together, not forcing the baby to bounce between us."

"Well, the baby won't be bouncing anywhere for quite some time. He or she will need to be with me since I'll be nursing."

"I have no desire to separate the baby from you, but no Italian court will decide to give you custody based on breastfeeding."

She gripped her hands tightly together to hold back the whisper of panic. She hadn't flown all this way to lose her child. She hadn't begun this trip to be told she'd have only partial custody, either.

In her heart, she believed that babies belonged with the mother. It was her mother who did all the heavy lifting when Charlotte was small. Well, her mother and the fleet of nannies and housekeepers who were employed to keep the family running.

She blinked hard, fighting emotion she didn't understand.

He shot her a swift glance. "You should have come to me right away, you know. You should have told me the moment you knew you were pregnant. Instead you've had all this time to imagine life the way you wanted it to be, versus what it must be."

"You don't have to want the baby," she said under her breath.

"But I do."

She turned away, glancing out at the river, and the light bouncing on the bridges and elegant historic buildings. "During the ultrasound, I was asked if I wanted to know the baby's gender, and I said I didn't, because it doesn't matter if I'm expecting a boy or girl. I'm simply excited about being a mom, and the goal is a healthy baby."

"Agreed," he said. "But that baby is going to need a family. A healthy family. Neither one of us can do that on our own."

Brando drove, concentrating on the road, and Charlotte watched the city suburbs give way to rolling hills of gold and green.

For the next forty minutes, Brando drove the narrow, winding road that connected Florence to Siena, a road famous for its scenic beauty through hills and valleys dotted with villages and vineyards, while Charlotte admired the beautiful landscape. This was the renowned Chianti Valley, an area famous for its wines, olive trees and medieval villages.

She knew about his estate, but had never been there, and she was curious about the undulating hills, and the picturesque villages, each with its own bell tower rising above tiled roofs.

They were between villages when a tire blew in a loud pop and the sports car pulled sharply right. Brando slowed, and parked on the shoulder of the road, before climbing out to inspect the damage.

"It's just the tire," he said, opening her car door to speak to her. "Stay put. I can change it while you're in there."

She watched him roll his sleeves higher on his arms. His arms were sculpted of corded muscle. His skin the loveliest shade of bronze. "I heard it was dangerous to do that," she said, remembering how his shoulders had been equally powerful, and his torso endless lean muscle.

"You'll be safer in the car than standing on this narrow road."

"But what about you?" she asked, shading her eyes to look up into his face.

"Nothing's going to happen to me. You're the one I'm worried about." He closed the door firmly and she turned in her seat to watch him go to the boot and pull out the spare tire, the jack and tools.

He made changing it look effortless—well, except for the part where he lay on the ground, partway under the car to check the jack's position, and then he was out again and the car was up, the lug bolts off, tire swapped, lug bolts replaced and car back down. Brando stowed the flat tire, dusted himself off and returned to the driver's seat, flashing her a wry smile. "Hope I didn't keep you waiting too long," he said.

His olive cheeks had a dusky flush and his eyes were bright from exertion, but he looked sexier than ever, and she thought a man who knew how to do things with his hands was incredibly appealing.

"That was impressive," she said, smiling at him as he buckled his seat belt.

"You must be easily impressed, then."

"Actually, I'm not. I have very high standards."

He shot her an amused glance. "Then how did I get you into my bed last New Year's Eve?"

It was her turn to blush, and she felt herself go hot all over. "Can we blame the champagne?"

"You weren't drinking that night. Everyone tried to hand you a glass of something. You refused."

"I rarely drink." She wrinkled her nose. "It's not that I don't like alcohol, but I'm a control freak."

"I see. You lost control, hated yourself for it and then promptly ghosted me."

"I didn't *ghost* you."

"What would you call it, then? No calls, no emails, no communication?"

"We didn't have sex to start a relationship. We had sex because we were attracted to each other and we were curious to see if it would be good."

One of his black brows lifted mockingly. "I hadn't realized I'd left you disappointed."

"You didn't. You know that night was incredible. But it wasn't something that we could do again. I was hired to work for your family, not bed the rebel son."

"I'm no longer the rebel son. I've become the good son."

"Then why do Enzo, Marcello and Livia all work together at the Ricci headquarters in Florence and you have your own office? And why are they no longer involved in the wineries, and you alone manage that arm of the Ricci business?"

He shrugged. "Because I have an affinity for the land, and they don't."

"Marcello told me you're the smartest of them all, but they worry about you doing your own thing."

"Because I don't do things by consensus, I do what I think is best. They don't like it—"

"Because you're the youngest?"

"And because you've met them. You know how it is. Too much discussion. Too much tension. It's a waste of time and energy. If something needs to be done, I'm going to do it. End of story."

"You don't feel isolated?"

"No. I love it. It's far better now that they are out of the fields and winery, and they can focus on fashion, and merchandising."

"And yet I saw the report Enzo had prepared for our meetings last August. Your wineries are outperforming, and outearning, what the three of them do...combined."

"Now it does. It wasn't always that way."

"But you have to be pleased."

"I'm not competitive, at least, not with them. I like to be successful, but not at their expense." He glanced at her, black lashes framing those startling silver eyes. "They're my older brothers and my sister. I look up to them. I respect them. I just want to do my part now—" He broke off, drew a breath, "It's time to do my part, to ensure my family's success."

It wasn't a villa, but a proper castle, she realized as they turned off the main road and began driving up a hill to the castle with a square tower in front of them, while tidy rows of grapes covered the hillsides.

"That's your home," she said, because it was the only building nearby, and what an impressive structure it was. The tower was made of stone, while the plastered walls were a soft creamy yellow, surrounded by tall stone exterior walls.

"It is," he agreed.

The *castello* was positioned on a hill with sweeping views of Val di Greve, and with access to both Florence and Siena, it had most likely been a strategic stronghold for centuries.

"From the square tower, it must date back to the eleven hundreds."

"There are some disagreements regarding the age of the *castello* itself, but historians all agree that the central tower is from the twelfth century. Some sources claim the castle as it is today dates from the early fourteen hundreds. We know from ancient records that the *castello* has been inhabited since 1456, and it was during that time period it earned its name, Castello Mare Scotti, for a descendent of the Medicis."

"When did you buy the property?"

"It's been almost ten years. The castle and grounds were a mess, in need of serious restoration, and while the vineyards were still producing grapes, they also needed to be replanted. Overhauling the orchards made sense—and those have become quite profitable. The restoration of the *castello* is more of a labor of love, an ode to Tuscany. I've lived many places now, but nowhere else is like this place. Chianti Valley is without a doubt home."

"More so than Florence?"

"I enjoy Florence. It's elegant and filled with art and history, but I've discovered I prefer the country over the city. My family had a big estate outside Florence when I was growing up, and my brothers have divided it between them, but that estate has never resonated with me, not the way Castello Marescotti resonates. From the first time I walked the property, I knew it was meant for me." Brando flashed a wry smile. "The family said I was crazy. Livia emailed me a half-dozen listings of available properties featuring palaces and villas in excellent condition, many with land attached, but none of them were right. Marescotti was mine. I often spend weeks at a time here. One day soon I hope to live here full-time."

"What about your house in Florence?"

"I'll still go for a special night, or a weekend, but once I have children—" He broke off and shot her a meaningful glance as he slowed to pass through the ten-foot stone walls with the huge iron gate. "I'd like to raise them where there is space to run and play."

Staff appeared as Brando parked. Someone claimed the luggage. Someone else took the car keys and then the car. A housekeeper ushered them through the front door, offering to show Charlotte to her room, but Brando said he'd take her himself.

Sunlight poured through the windows flanking the front door, and the staircase rose in the middle of the great hall, the staircase three levels of dark gleaming wood against pale yellow walls. Framed oil canvases hung on the walls while an enormous Venetian glass chandelier cast sparkling light everywhere.

She followed Brando up a flight of stairs to the second floor. They walked down the hall to the second door on the left. Her bedroom was luxurious as well as spacious, with plastered walls and thick dark beams set into the ceiling. The rose silk curtains framed tall windows, and the bed was covered with a matching silk coverlet. Fresh roses filled a vase next to the bed, and more roses nestled in a low bowl on the antique dressing table.

"Would you like a brief tour of the house and gardens?" Brando asked. "Or are you too tired?"

"Not too tired. I'd love to see your place. I heard so much about it last fall."

They exited her bedroom, stepping back into the hallway, which was sunny and bright thanks to a trio of tall windows lining the wall. The windows overlooked fertile vineyards and tidy orchards.

"How much of this land is yours?" she asked, pausing at one of the hall windows.

"Almost everything you can see from this spot." He pointed to a distant hill topped with another castle. "See that *castello*? That is my nearest neighbor, and his property starts at the bottom of his hill and continues for one hundred and ten acres that way. Everything from here, to that hill, is mine."

"How many acres do you have?"

"A little over two thousand, but it's in chunks and clusters as I've purchased available property in the valley."

Her eyebrows arched. "That is significant land for this area, isn't it?"

"I've been buying land when I can. Most of it is devoted to grapes, but not all. I also have a large olive orchard, and we have bees, and produce honey, too."

He led her back downstairs through the reception rooms and grand salons and smaller sitting rooms, as well as through the dining room, and the kitchen staffed with a head chef and an assistant. They walked through kitchen gardens, their shoes crunching the gravel paths, before entering a small orchard with fruit trees. At the back of the fruit orchard were the beehives, and they found one of Brando's gardeners, who also was the chief beekeeper, just finishing repairing the rain cover on one of the hives. Brando greeted him warmly and introduced Charlotte before they continued, returning to the path with the worn tiles. The smooth red-tiled path led them away from the house to a small chapel with its own square bell tower. They peeked into the chapel with its stained glass and dark wooden pews, before he led her back down the path, cutting through rose gardens and a topiary garden to end up at an enormous infinity pool with a jaw-dropping view of the valley. Elegant wrought iron loungers lined one side of the pool while a fountain happily splashed away in a far corner, creating tinkling sounds.

The valley was that of dark green rolling hills and picturesque villages and grapes. The terrain was more rugged than Napa, with high mountains in the distance. "You have a bit of paradise here," she said.

"I'm quite partial to it. I focus well here. In fact, I enjoy my work so much that it doesn't feel like work."

"That's the best sort of work, when it feels more like a passion."

"Do you feel that way about your work?"

"Sometimes. It depends on the clients. And the crisis." She flashed a smile. "Sometimes the crisis element overwhelms everything else and all I feel is adrenaline."

"Did you feel that way working with my family?"

"No. The Riccis are pragmatic. None of you liked the bad press, and you were able to come together to downplay the succession issue." She made a face. "Not that the issue has gone away. It's just smoothed over for the time being."

"I think we've at least begun to whittle away at the issue. We aren't burying our heads in the sand anywhere. Something has to be done."

"But you personally don't think Enzo's son is the one to lead the Ricci company in the future."

"I think he should be involved in management, but Antonio isn't a visionary, and he's overly cautious, which leads to a fear of making decisions. You can't have your CEO afraid to make a decision."

"And what of Marcello's and Livia's kids? Anyone there look promising?"

"Livia's daughter, Adriana, is brilliant. She's strategic and has this rather dazzling ability to 'see' the future while very much coping with issues of today. My vote would be for Adriana, but that won't be popular with my brothers. They both have sons and they're both grooming their sons to head the company." He paused and looked down at her. "And who knows what our child's strengths will be, but I'm hopeful he or she will also embrace the family, as loud and fierce and complicated as we are."

"Yet you all love each other," she said after a moment. "I think that is the thing that struck me most. You quarrel rather passionately, but that's because you all care so much." Her family was the opposite. The quarreling wasn't warm and loving. The quarreling was incredibly divisive, so divisive that Charlotte was more comfortable with her stepbrothers and sisters than her own siblings.

He shrugged. "We're family. Family sticks together."

Or not.

He looked at her, silver gaze assessing. "You don't agree?"

"My family isn't as neat and tidy as yours, so I'm not sure how I feel about 'family.' It's not a simple question, nor a simple answer."

His expression eased, and he smiled. "Then how about I pose a simple question. Are you hungry? Lunch should be served soon."

"I am hungry," she admitted. "Lately I feel like I'm always hungry."

"Then let's walk back to the house, and you can freshen up before we meet on the terrace for lunch."

Brando escorted her back to the sprawling *castello*, where he left her at the foot of the stairs—on her insistence, as she didn't need to be walked all the way to her bedroom door—but as she climbed the stairs to the second floor, she couldn't help thinking of what Brando had said when they'd first arrived, that Castello Marescotti is where he'd want to raise his children, because there would be room for them to run and play. He was right, there was plenty of room here, both indoors and out. The stone house was huge, almost too big for a game of hide-and-seek, but she'd been raised in such a place herself and had thought nothing of the grandness, or the sheer amount of space. It's what she knew. It was home.

In her room, she took a brush to her hair, combing through the long blond strands until they were smooth, and then touched up her makeup. As she reapplied her lipstick, Charlotte tried to imagine this house as her baby's home and felt an odd prickle of pain and her hand shook. She had to draw a breath and steady her hand before putting the cap on the lipstick. It wasn't that this grand medieval house wasn't comfortable, because the interior was stylish and yet welcoming, a place both grown-ups and children would be at ease, but rather it was the idea of the baby being here without her…that her baby would have a whole life without her…

Sudden tears stung her eyes and she blinked hard, clearing her vision. She wasn't usually emotional, and yet all she felt right now were emotions, strong, intense, overwhelming.

She loved her unborn child rather desperately, and every fiber of her being wanted to protect the baby. But how could she do that if she wasn't with him or her?

How could she bring a child into the world and then not be part of his or her life…even part-time?

She put away her lipstick and slid the makeup bag and hairbrush into the top dresser of the pretty vanity, and then squared her shoulders. She could do this with Brando. She could be civil, and calm, and make him understand that she wasn't going to let a baby grow up without her. She didn't know the answer to "sharing" the baby, she just knew she was going to be with her child full-time, end of story.

CHAPTER FOUR

BRANDO WAITED FOR Charlotte on the terrace, the sun warm overhead as he stood at the balcony overlooking the valley. It was perfect weather for lunch al fresco, the temperature warm, the air fragrant, smelling of roses, citrus blossoms and jasmine. The table was set for two, and a lush bouquet of pale pink and creamy white antique roses created a charming centerpiece, especially when paired with the fine china and delicate Venetian stemware.

It was a table setting that hinted at romance, but there was nothing romantic about his intentions. Brando had never been a man of romance—he was far too carnal, far too practical. He loved women and loved sex, but so far, he'd been careful to avoid commitments, much less serious entanglements.

And yet despite his best efforts to avoid entanglements, he was facing one now, an entanglement with lifelong implications.

He'd known that one day he'd have children—Italians were family oriented, and he had a wicked soft spot for his nieces and nephews, who made it clear they adored him—but marriage and children was down the road, far, far down the road, because marriage was forever. Marriage required complete commitment, as well as a suitable partner who one could grow old with, and hopefully, still like decades later.

His parents had had such a marriage. His parents married in their twenties, and had just celebrated their sixtieth wedding anniversary when his father passed away. Heartbroken, his mother had almost immediately moved to her widowed sister's house in Cinque Terre, where she and her sister found happiness being under the same roof. They missed their husbands but found endless opportunities to see their children and grandchildren.

Livia and Enzo had grumbled about their mother moving to the coast, to a place that wasn't easy to reach, but Marcello agreed with Brando that it was good for their mother to have an identity of her own, that she needed to have adventures and fun, adventures that had nothing to do with the rest of them.

Brando smiled thinking of his mother. She was a spitfire, full of endless energy, and she was always happy to see her family, but he respected her for not wanting to sit around her house, just mourning the death of her husband, and waiting for death to come. Life was meant to be lived. Life was meant to have passion, and gusto, and if anyone in the family had gusto, it was his mother.

But he also knew what his mother would say if he knew he'd gotten a woman pregnant. Her first question would be, "How will you make this right?" Not because a pregnancy was shameful, but a pregnancy represented life, and love, and family. He didn't think of himself as a traditionalist, but the idea of someone, *anyone*, having his child and raising that child far from him made his skin crawl. Maybe Charlotte was comfortable picturing a world where her baby—*their* baby, he corrected himself—shuttled back and forth between two homes, but he wasn't.

He knew her family had numerous marriages, divorces and out-of-wedlock babies in it. They took the idea of commitment far more loosely than his family did. There hadn't been a divorce in his family for generations. Nor had there been a baby born out of wedlock.

One of his older brothers had married when his girlfriend was pregnant, and it had been a rather hastily arranged wedding, but they were still together, and had added three other children besides that first unplanned pregnancy.

Brando hadn't been thinking of marriage, nor had he thought he was ready to settle down, but if Charlotte was pregnant, this was serious. This was a game changer. This impacted everything. Either she would agree to give him custody of the baby—which he didn't see her ever doing—or she would agree to marry him. Those were the only two options he saw. He wasn't about to have his firstborn raised in a bohemian household in California, or at one of the sprawling estates owned by her family in England. Her family seemed to spend as much time in England as they did in France and that was not acceptable, not for a Ricci. His family was Italian, and proud of their heritage. He wanted his child—son or daughter—to be raised immersed in his culture, his language, his family.

Bottom line, he wanted his child to be part of his family.

And put like that, it did make him sound conservative, and old-world. But the Riccis were family oriented, and family came first, and last, and they understood what it meant to stick together, through thick and thin. It wasn't that her family or culture didn't count, but her culture was a mishmash of English, American, French, and then there were those years from the Swiss boarding school, years where he suspected young women were taught how to snare the world's most eligible bachelors, rather than how to live a successful, independent life.

Charlotte, though, was probably the exception. She'd started her own business and had created a name for herself. She was financially independent, and successful. She'd be a good wife. Once he convinced her it was the right thing to do.

He thought of her, stubborn, proud, confident—and then just like that, she was there, stepping through the glass doors out into the Tuscany sunshine, blond hair spilling down her back, a hint of rose in her cheek, fire in her eyes—and he knew it would take some convincing, to get her on the same page.

She wasn't going to want to marry him, but having weighed his options, it was the only real option before them.

Lunch was leisurely, with small courses being replaced by other courses, and the portions were perfectly sized so that Charlotte enjoyed everything as much as she could, considering Brando kept watching her with an intensity that she found dizzying. Every movement reflected his physical strength and grace. He was not a man of leisure. One didn't get a body like his without hard activity. She had a sudden flash of memory, of his hips arching against hers, his body filling her so completely that she wanted nothing more than to be his, again and again.

The vividness of the memory, the picture of his beautiful naked body above her, filled her with heat and a breathlessness that made it impossible to take another bite of her custard dessert.

She pushed the small plate away, hot, flustered, confused, and put a hand to her hot cheek, as if to cool herself.

"Is it too warm in the sun?" Brando asked, immediately noting her gesture. "Would you prefer to sit in the shade? We can move to the umbrella—"

"I'm fine. The sun is gorgeous."

He didn't appear convinced. "I don't want to fatigue you."

"I'm pregnant, not eighty, Brando."

"Yes, you're pregnant," he said darkly. "Which is why I won't have you overly tired. Perhaps we should go inside—"

"I'm *fine*. Trust me."

"You're flushed."

Yes, because I'm thinking about making love to you. Thinking about your body. Thinking about the amazing things you did with your body...

She didn't say it, though, but she blushed, exquisitely aware of him.

"If you truly are comfortable where we are, I think it's time we talked about why you've come to Italy, and what we're going to do." Brando's deep voice was firm, his gaze direct as it met hers.

"I suggest we marry. Soon. A simple ceremony, followed by an intimate dinner with our immediate family—"

"Excuse me?" she interrupted, brow creasing.

"The sooner the better," he concluded.

"Your wife?" She stared at him aghast. "Please tell me I'm misunderstanding you."

"No. You are understanding me perfectly."

"I am not going to marry you."

"Why not?" he retorted calmly.

"There's no reason for us to marry. We're not living in the Dark Ages, or the Victorian times.

There is no reason we can't have a child without being married—"

"There is in my family."

"Maybe your family needs to adapt, then. Maybe it's time the Riccis evolved."

"It's not just about my family's values, or morality," he answered. "It's about the business. Our child won't have any hopes of heading the family business if we're not married."

"Well, I sincerely doubt our child would want to head your family business, not if it's that archaic." She gave him a long look. "And I know your family is archaic. It's why I was called in to mediate in the first place. The Riccis still live in the nineteenth century, but it's time they caught up with the rest of the world. Children do just fine in single-parent homes. Children thrive—"

"When raised in a stable home, with two loving stable parents."

She eyed him for a long moment. "You and I are stable, and we will be loving parents. But it's not necessary to be in the same house together. In fact, that's asking for disaster. I can guarantee that will create more instability than anything."

"Why?"

"We're not meant to be together, Brando, and regarding a single home, you don't live in just one house. You bounce between your properties, never in one place long."

"But you've already heard me say that this place

is home, and this is where I intend to raise my children."

"You're not settled here yet, and babies are adaptable. Obviously it's different once children are in school, but that's years from now. Five or six years."

"I hadn't planned on settling down quite yet, but your pregnancy changes everything. It changes both of us. I'm prepared to make the necessary changes." He hesitated a beat. "Are you?"

She felt her shoulders rise, and a quick hot retort rush to her tongue, but she held the words back and forced herself to count to five, and then ten. "I already have. I'm preparing a nursery in my home. I've begun taking birthing classes."

"All without me?"

She choked on an uneasy laugh. "I'm not planning my future around you, no."

"You should be. I'm planning my future around you, or more correctly, I'm planning my future with you."

If her heart wasn't racing she'd get up and move. Flee. But as it was, she didn't feel steady enough to even get up and walk. "I don't think we're on the same page," she said hoarsely.

"*Cara*, my love, children need security, traditions and a familiar routine."

She suppressed a shiver at the husky rasp in his voice, as well as the endearments. She wasn't his darling, or his love, and she hated that he sounded so reasonable, so patient, when everything in her screamed in protest. "That's where we don't see eye to eye, Brando, as I had very two very different families and very different traditions with each family, and it didn't hurt me. If anything, it was good for me. I learned to be flexible, and adaptable."

"You say that now, but I'm sure you felt pain when your parents divorced, and then your mother remarried and moved you to California."

"It was a change, and yes, it was hard being ten with chaos all around me, but I'm stronger because I've had to deal with challenging circumstances."

"But if you had your way, is that what you'd wish on your child? Challenging circumstances? Or would you want to protect him, or her—"

"Now you're just being unfair. I would always want to protect my baby. I want to do what's best for the baby, which is why I'm here, trying to include you, but there's a big difference between including you and becoming your doormat!"

"How is marriage making you a doormat?"

"Because it's giving up everything I want, and need, to do what you think is best. But I don't believe it's necessary for us to marry, and I most definitely don't believe it's the best thing for us. We can provide stable homes independently of the other. You provide a home here in Italy, and I'll provide one in LA—"

"You can't possibly be serious about raising our child in Los Angeles."

"What's wrong with Los Angeles?"

"What is right about Los Angeles?"

She pressed her lips together, frustrated and unwilling to say more. She counted to ten, and then she couldn't remain silent any longer, and blurted, "There is much to like about Italy, and much to love about Tuscany, but you're a little too smug about being Italian—"

"I'm proud of my heritage."

"But it's not the only heritage in play here. I have my own."

"You've run away from yours. You left it behind. You're just like everyone else that has run to Los Angeles, looking to reinvent themselves."

His scorn stung and she bit into her lower lip, trying not to focus on his criticism. He was fighting for a place in their child's life. He was fighting to be included. She understood that. She respected that. But he was giving her no middle ground and middle ground is what she needed. "There is beauty in reinvention," she said quietly. "And beauty in change. I appreciate you wanting to do the right thing by offering to marry me, but I must decline, must most adamantly decline. I will not marry because it's the morally right thing. If I marry it's because I'm in love and want to spend the rest of my life with someone, rather than being trapped with someone out of duty or misplaced obligation."

"Now that is old-fashioned."

"To marry for love?"

"Love marriages end in divorce when the dopamine fades. You and I both know that. Children can help parents bond, and marriages can last because of oxytocin. We make a choice, and then choose to be committed, and we have a marriage that endures."

"For a moment, I thought you were speaking of grafting grapevines. That is another asexual propagation technique."

"Yes, but I believe our procreation technique was sexual. I believe you're pregnant because we couldn't get enough of each other."

True, true, true.

Charlotte closed her eyes, held her breath and prayed for something witty to say, because right now she just felt trapped.

"We still have two days," Brando said quietly, "two days before you fly to London. Let's say no more now, and let you have some time to yourself. We can discuss this again at dinner."

Her eyes opened and she looked at him a long moment before she gave her head a short, regretful shake. He was beautiful, and fascinating, but not the man she'd marry. Not a man she could plan a life with, either. He loved women, loved sex, loved his freedom. He'd be a terrible husband, and he'd break her heart because she wouldn't be able to share him, nor would she be able to forgive him for being in other women's beds. "My feelings won't change."

"Neither will the facts. We're having a baby. We have to put aside our differences—"

"I don't think we can."

"Let's leave it for now. We have tonight."

In her bedroom, Charlotte curled up in a chair near the window, pressed her fist to her mouth and stared out the window at the valley trying to calm herself and yet unable to relax, annoyed by Brando's high-handedness, and frustrated by his inability to listen to what she wanted and needed.

This was why she didn't date powerful men, or powerful, wealthy men, and this was why she didn't want to become part of a powerful man's family… or any family that made edicts and rules and told her how she was supposed to live and behave. She wanted to be herself. She wanted to be her own person.

How did she become so good at handling family strife? Because she'd grown up in it. Immersed in it. And would have drowned in it if she hadn't figured out how to rise above.

The point was, she understood family dynamics, and family politics. But just because she understood it didn't mean she wanted to spend her future answering to others. It was bad enough that she still had her own family to contend with, but to marry Brando, and to suddenly have to deal with the Ricci family, as well?

No.

It wasn't going to happen.

His family were not bad people, and she'd enjoyed them as an outside consultant, but Riccis were very strong and opinionated, and passionate, and forceful with their thoughts and feelings. Her family, on the other hand, were quieter, and judgmental, and distantly disapproving. One still had to measure up, but the interactions were different, and the expectations were communicated differently. She didn't know what was worse: the fierce, expressive discussions that took place in passionate families, or the cool, disapproving silence of her family. Either way, she preferred the calm of living alone, on her own terms, able to make the decisions that were right for her.

During dinner Charlotte felt as if she was on pins and needles, waiting for Brando to launch into another persuasive speech about why marriage was the right choice for them, but he didn't. Instead he asked her how much she knew about the wines of Tuscany, and when she said she knew very little other than Chianti was considered the most popular red wine from Tuscany, he gave her an interesting history of winemaking in Tuscany, explaining that Sangiovese, the most commonly plated red grape, and the basis for Chianti Classico wines, was such an ancient grape in Italy that many considered it indigenous to the area. "It's a grape that has a very long growing season, budding early, and then needs time to ripen. In the industry, we say it's slow to ripen."

"Not all grapes are slow to ripen, then?" she asked.

"We have mutual friends in Napa Valley, and their Chardonnay and Pinot Noir are both early ripening grapes. Cab, Merlot, Sangiovese are late varieties."

"Is that what brought you to California last year?"

"No." His gaze met hers and held. "You did."

"Me?"

"Mmm-hmm. I'd hoped to see you again."

She felt herself flush. "We agreed there would be just that one night."

"Most women don't mean it."

She grew hotter, her skin hot and prickly across her cheekbones, her lips tingling, too. And just the tingle in her lips made her remember how good his mouth had felt on hers, and how his kisses had drawn her in, pulling her under, seducing her like nothing she'd ever known before. "I'm not sure how to respond to that."

"You're remarkably good at compartmentalizing."

But ah, she wasn't, and she hadn't found it easy to put him behind her. She'd felt almost desperate with desire, and she'd craved him for weeks after her return to Southern California. The desire and her emotions had been so intense they'd scared her, making her feel alien even to herself. In the end, being with him that night hadn't been a release, but a bond, and now the ties to that bond were tightening. Her stomach did an uncomfortable little flip and she forced herself to respond, feigning a cavalier attitude she didn't feel. "You mean, good at compartmentalizing for a woman?"

"I'm not sexist."

"Oh, you most definitely are. You're the one expecting me to move here. You're the one that won't even consider other arrangements."

"Nothing is in stone. I'm open to discussion, open to suggestions. How should we make this work, *cara*?"

Again, she bristled inwardly at the endearment. He said them so easily, dropping them like overripe cherries, even as he neatly turned the tables on her. "There is no simple solution. It's one of the reasons I've waited to come to you. I needed to accept what's happening, and then problem-solve. And I'm here now, because I believe that at least for the baby's first year, the baby should be with me—"

"Then how will our baby bond with me?" he interrupted, his expression still pleasant but there was a new, steely edge to his voice.

"Fathers bond with their children later… They're never fond of the baby stage and tend to feel useless until babies are weaned and able to have more independence and mobility."

Brando looked at her for a moment before laughing, and not just a little laugh, but a big, deep laugh as if he'd never heard anything half so amusing. "I don't know where you get your information from, but it's wrong."

"It's common knowledge."

"Is it?"

Again, he made her hackles rise. "My father had no use for babies. My brothers are useless until the toddler stage, but even then, they hate it when the children cry for Mummy."

"Maybe it's cultural, then, because my father was very hands-on, from day one. My brothers all helped with the night feedings by changing diapers, bringing the newborn to their wives and then burping the newborn before returning to bed. Marcello and his wife have a young baby now, and they're in the middle of the sleepless-night phase. Marcello is exhausted but he said he wouldn't trade this stage for anything. It's when he feels closest to the bambino, and the most needed."

His words filled her with a strange yearning feeling, which was so strange since just a moment ago she felt fierce and angry. She hated the rioting within her making herself feel as if she were a living kaleidoscope. "You paint an idyllic picture."

"Well, I've left out the colic, and the baby that won't sleep at night, but insists on napping all day, or the exhaustion from trying to cope with an inconsolable infant who won't stop screaming."

She just looked at him, unable to think of a thing

to say because it struck her for the first time that he might know more about newborns than she did.

"It's easier to parent as a team. I think we should work as a team," he added. "I think we'd be most successful as parents that way."

She suddenly needed air. She needed to move and breathe and she couldn't do it in the dining room, as elegant as it was. "Would you mind terribly if we stepped outside? I'm feeling overly warm."

"Let's step outside and walk a bit. It might be a little cool, though."

"I'm sure it'd feel good."

It was cooler outside, but not cold, and there was a light breeze that carried the fragrance of flowers, freshly cut grass and warm soil. It was rich and ripe and pungent and Charlotte breathed deeply, drawing the layered scent in, reminded of her family's country house in Sussex.

"How are you feeling now?" Brando asked her as they walked along the pea gravel path that led from the house and into a long, rectangular walled garden, the pale gray stone walls lined with neatly pruned boxwoods, the center dominated by an ornate fountain that looked as if it had been there for hundreds of years, and two ornate flower beds. The light was just now fading, painting the garden shades of lavender and plum.

"A little better," she said.

"That doesn't sound very convincing," he replied.

She didn't answer, and he said nothing. They walked the length of the walled garden in thoughtful silence, and then did another lap, completing a full circle of the garden.

"I'm just scared," Charlotte blurted, stopping next to the fountain. "I feel like everything is moving faster and faster, and I feel like I'm losing control."

"You're entering the final trimester. It won't be long until the baby arrives, and that is a loss of control. Everything will be different, for both of us."

The baby gave a kick just then and she inhaled and put a hand to the side of her bump.

"Moving?" he asked.

She nodded. Impulsively she reached for his hand, and placed it where hers had been, pressing his palm to the spot she'd felt the kick. For a moment nothing happened, and then it happened, a swift, little kick, or stretch. She looked up into his face to see if he'd felt it.

His jaw had firmed, and his lips pressed, but his silver gaze softened, and there was a look of wonder in his expression. *"Sorprendente,"* he murmured. *Amazing.*

Her eyes burned, hot and gritty, and she blinked, chasing away the stinging sensation, but she couldn't erase the aching lump in her throat. Quickly, she let go of his hand, suddenly self-conscious, aware that she'd reached for him, creating an intimacy neither of them wanted.

"I'm glad you're here," he said huskily. "I'm glad you came now, so that I can be part of this. Thank you."

Her heart squeezed and she felt more of that terrible pain —yearning coupled with fear, longing layered with anger. Feelings were messy business. She preferred order and structure.

As if he could read her mind, he tipped her chin up, studying her face in the soft light of the rising moon. "Neither of us has absolute control," he said. "But then, no one has absolute control."

And then he dropped his head, his mouth covering hers, and kissed her. She'd imagined that maybe his kiss now would feel platonic, or reassuring, but no, the kiss was just as shocking and scorching as it had been New Year's Eve when his lips made her feel as if she'd touched a live wire, electricity coursing through her.

He must have felt her shuddering response because he drew her closer, his lips moving across hers, deepening the kiss. She thought she'd remembered the pleasure, but this was even more intense, more sensual, and she welcomed the pressure of his mouth, and his hand sliding from her waist down her hip. She leaned into him, giving herself over to him, and when he parted her lips, and his tongue swept the inside of her soft swollen bottom lip, she couldn't contain her sigh, or the desire humming through her.

He caught her soft lip between his teeth, and then

his tongue stroked the inside of her mouth, reminding her of how his hips had moved as he'd thrust into her, filling her, making her body come alive.

She was coming alive now, feverishly alive, and she clutched Brando, holding on, legs weak, heart pounding, veins full of honey and fire.

Then his head lifted and he gazed down into her eyes. "I suggest we marry as soon as possible."

Charlotte staggered back a step, dazed, senses swimming. "What?"

"I'll look into the paperwork tomorrow."

"Brando, no." She moved back another step, legs trembling, tension rippling through her. "Marriage isn't the answer, it isn't. There must be another way to make this work. I'll get an apartment in Florence…something not far from yours."

"We should be together, under one roof."

"Then give me a suite of rooms in your house. We'll be roommates."

"That will never work. There's too much chemistry between us. We'll drive each other mad."

"I'm not going to rush into anything. We have time. We have months."

"Let's not tempt fate."

"Months," she repeated firmly, smashing her panic, even as she turned around and started back to the *castello*, her gaze fixed on the tall, magnificent house glimmering with soft yellow light.

CHAPTER FIVE

THE MORNING SUN shone brightly, warming Brando's back as he walked from the house to the vineyard. The dark soil beneath his feet smelled fresh, the air around him fragrant. Summer was coming, and then it'd be fall. Brando was glad to be back on his estate, and he never felt more peace than when he was here, close to the vineyards, able to walk amid the vines. He checked clusters of grapes as he walked between the tidy rows. It looked like an excellent crop this year and he anticipated a good harvest come September.

But that wasn't all that would happen. By the time the grapes were harvested, he would be a father.

He hadn't quite yet become accustomed to the thought. It was still exciting, surprising. Even a little overwhelming. He hadn't been ready to settle down, hadn't imagined starting a family for another few years. Because the Riccis didn't divorce, they tended to marry late, and he was no exception. He'd planned on marrying in his mid to late thirties, but God had a different plan, and he was good with that.

Charlotte, he knew, wasn't.

Charlotte saw obstacles where he saw solutions. He wasn't worried, not yet. He'd find a way to make her understand, but it would mean he needed time, and there wasn't much time, not if she intended to be on a flight to London tomorrow.

He paused at the next row, fingers lightly brushing a leaf, and then the cluster of grapes beneath.

Time together was what they needed. If she was determined to still go to London tomorrow, then he'd go with her.

Better yet, he'd fly her there himself.

None of Charlotte's clients knew she was pregnant, and none of them knew she was in Italy, either. She woke up to dozens of new emails in her inbox, and her phone showed an alarming number of new texts and voice messages needing attention.

Work was good, she told herself, as she sat with her laptop at the breakfast table, responding to emails she could answer now, and making note of what she'd need to do to get back to people.

She had to survive only another day here, she told herself, and then she'd be in England, with her family—not that any of them knew she was coming, in part because she wasn't sure where she should go. But she didn't have to have that figured out yet. Tomorrow was tomorrow, today was today, and she'd devote the rest of her morning to work, and then eventually she'd have to face Brando, and hopefully by the time she did, she'd be more sanguine about the kiss.

The kiss.

Her fingers hovered over her keyboard as heat washed through her. The kiss…

Brando still had such an effect on her. There was something so elemental about him, them, and she couldn't resist him, not physically. Emotionally, that was a different matter. Emotionally, all she had to do was remember Louisa at the door of his Florence house, practically naked, clearly having come to the door from his bed, and that memory still made her recoil.

She knew she couldn't judge him for having others—there was no relationship between them. But how could she make the leap from "nothing" to wife?

It didn't make sense. She couldn't wrap her head around it…or her heart. And for marriage, she needed her heart.

She closed her laptop and pushed it away before crossing her arms over her chest, frustrated and indignant. It was a mistake coming to Florence to see Brando, and an even bigger mistake agreeing to come to this house in the country with him because everywhere she looked, it was his world. She didn't belong here, and she felt trapped right now, trapped in his big, sprawling *castello*, trapped by the beautiful pastoral views, trapped in his world that was both seductive, and consuming.

Brando wasn't like anyone else she had ever known, and she didn't know how to deal with him. She felt hormonal, and restless, agitated and confused. She should have just stayed in California and gone to her yoga class and eaten her healthy salads and worked at her desk and sent him a message that they needed to talk, that she had something important to tell him.

He would have come to see her.

She could have stayed put and made him do the traveling. Why didn't she?

That was easy. She'd secretly wanted the element of surprise. She'd wanted to discover for herself who he really was, not who she imagined him to be. She wanted facts. The truth. Because one night together wasn't anything, one night of sex was just a fantasy. After she'd returned to Los Angeles, she'd built him up in her mind, too, made him special, and wonderful…almost mythic…and she knew it couldn't all be true, that he couldn't really be everything she'd made him out to be. And so, she'd arrived in his world unannounced, shown up on his doorstep to see what she would see—not the fantasy, but the man.

And the man had a famous model in his bed.

The man probably had famous models frequently in his bed. But, why shouldn't he? He was ridiculously wealthy, and impossibly handsome, and he made love like a god.

He'd made her feel things she didn't know she could feel, and he'd made her hope—as impossible as it was—that she was different. Special.

Seeing Louisa on his doorstep dispelled that hope. Charlotte wasn't special, or unique. What they'd done…experienced… New Year's Eve was no different from what he'd done, and shared, with countless other women. Unwittingly she thought of her family, and the affairs—hushed as they were—and the lack of commitment. Both of her parents had been unfaithful. Both of them had found it impossible to honor their wedding vows. If she married Brando, she'd be living with someone who wasn't that different from her father, and it filled her with pain.

But maybe pain was good. Maybe it was better this way, better to deal in facts.

Fact one: she was pregnant.

Fact two: the baby was due in three months.

Fact three: Brando Ricci, Italian tycoon, was the father.

Fact four: Brando didn't love her, but she, Charlotte Parks, might just be a little in love with him…

Footsteps sounded and she glanced up, hoping it was the housekeeper with her cappuccino. She'd had one earlier with breakfast but still craved another cup. Instead it was Brando, and he was carrying a tall bottle of water and a glass.

He twisted off the cap on the bottle and filled the glass with sparkling water before placing the glass in front of her. "Too much caffeine isn't good for the baby," he said. "Water is better for both of you."

"I didn't sleep well. I can't wake up."

"Go for a swim. That will be far more refreshing, and healthier, too."

"I'm not interested in squeezing myself into a bathing suit."

"There is no one to see. You'll have complete privacy."

"I have too much work to do, and sadly, I didn't bring a suit."

He dropped into a chair at the table. "Is there anything I can help you with?"

"No. You've done quite enough, thank you."

"Giving you water instead of coffee?"

"No, getting me pregnant. I think I'll handle everything else from here on out." She shifted in her chair, and drew a slow breath, trying to calm the butterflies in her middle and the tightness in her chest. Just his appearance set her heart racing, and now that he was seated close, she felt breathless. Because this was also a fact—her body liked him, very much.

And then she forced herself to remember Louisa, and Louisa was sleeping with him, and Louisa was his, or vice versa. But the point was, just two days ago he was with Louisa and now he was proposing marriage and the whole thing was ludicrous, and more than a little disturbing.

"How can you suggest marriage when you're still romantically involved with other women?" she said bluntly, unable to hold the words back. "And how can I possibly think marriage is an option when just days ago Louisa opened your door, practically naked?"

"I thought we talked about this."

"She answered your front door."

"She's a free spirit. She knew I didn't want her to, so she ran downstairs before I could."

"You like that?"

"She's playful. Fun."

Charlotte closed her eyes, aware that she was nothing like free spirit Louisa. In fact, Charlotte was the exact opposite of Louisa, and Charlotte couldn't imagine being wild and outrageous. From an early age, she'd recoiled from drawing attention...doing anything outside the norm. And the one time she took a risk, it had been a calculated risk, but still a risk, and Charlotte had ended up pregnant.

"I've told you this already. Louisa and I are not together," Brando said patiently. "There is nothing serious between us. She was in Florence and we met and had dinner—"

"Had sex."

"Yes."

"Probably lots of it."

He leaned forward abruptly, closing the distance between them. "Charlotte, what are you doing?"

There was a bite in his voice and she shook her

head, feeling sick. "This is all wrong," she murmured, looking anywhere but at him. "Every bit of it."

"You must stop thinking about Louisa. She's not part of this equation. No one is, but us. She is completely out of the picture"

She shook her head again, feeling even more frantic. "I can't have your baby. I can't. You will never be faithful. Never be mine. Never—" She broke off and jumped up, neatly sidestepping his hand to escape to the other side of the balcony. "What a mess this all is."

He rose from his chair and followed her. "What's going on? What's happening?"

"I'm just realizing that I've been living in a fantasy world. I've been pretending it's just the baby and me, but it's not. There is you, and you don't fit into my life or my plan. Last night you said we should marry. You said we should raise the baby together, married, but how? It'd never work. You're a bachelor. A virtual playboy—"

"I object. I'm not a playboy and have never been that."

"You have lots of sex with lots of women."

"When I'm in a committed relationship, I'm only with that woman. But if I'm not in a relationship, and I'm attracted to a woman, and she's attracted to me, we might go to bed together. Why not? Sex isn't bad, or dirty. It's physical, it's pleasurable. It's a form of communication and connection—"

"But I don't have sex with every man that is appealing. I don't just make love because I'm attracted to him."

"You did with me."

"And what a mistake that was," she retorted grimly.

He stood in front of her, hands on his lean hips, studying her. "You didn't think so at the time," he said after a long moment.

"I regretted it almost immediately," she answered, glancing at him, and then away, because it was too unnerving to meet his penetrating gaze. "I flew home kicking myself the entire way."

"That must have been a very painful flight," he said deadpan.

She rolled her eyes. "Of course you'd make a joke about it. You don't know me, and you don't understand the first thing about me, because if you did, you wouldn't have suggested marriage as if it were a cure-all. Marriage wouldn't make anything better, Brando. It would make everything worse."

"Explain."

"I just have no desire to be married, much less marry someone who I'm not compatible with. We had chemistry, but you have chemistry with every woman—"

"That's not true."

"And you enjoy your freedom, and the opportunity to be with different women, and I refuse to be the one who takes that freedom from you. You like being a bachelor, so be a bachelor. You can be a bachelor and a father. It's done all the time."

"Not in my family."

"Well, welcome to the twenty-first century, Ricci family."

He ignored the jab. "I was happy being single, but I will also be happy being married."

"I won't be."

"You don't know that, because you haven't even truly considered the suggestion. You've decided outright it's not for you—"

"Because it's not."

"But don't you think that's a little immature? Can you try to have an open mind? We're having a baby, and we need to come together for our child. I think you're using me as an excuse. I've told you I'm ready, and nothing will change my mind now."

Charlotte looked away, his words weighing heavily on her, eating away at her conscience and heart. She did want what was best for the baby, but the only reason Brando was suggesting marriage was for the baby. Not because he cared for her, and not because he thought it would be good for her, but it would be good for the baby, and the Ricci family name.

In Los Angeles she felt sure of herself, and confident of her place in life. Here…

Here she wasn't Charlotte Parks, but a woman carrying Brando Ricci's baby, the baby who would be his heir.

His heir.

Not hers.

"I liked my life as it was," she said finally. "And I don't think it's selfish or immature to say that I'm a better person on my own. Being independent has been good for me. Being able to be who I want to be, versus what others project onto me, has allowed me to become the me that is successful, and happy." She could feel his gaze on her and she glanced over her shoulder and looked at him. "At the same time, I'm aware that we must come up with some kind of solution, find some middle ground, but marriage isn't it."

"I didn't realize you're so opposed to marriage."

"Not opposed to marriage in general, but opposed to me marrying out of some archaic idea that marriage solves problems. Marriage doesn't solve problems. Marriage creates problems."

"If we were madly in love, would you still feel the same way?"

For some reason his question, in that slightly mocking inflection, made her smile. "I don't know. But then, I've never been madly in love. Have you?"

He moved to her side and leaned against the stone balustrade. "I don't think I've even been in love, period." He looked out toward the valley, his gaze on the horizon. "At least not the way you describe. I've had long and close relationships with women, relationships I cherished, but there was never a sense, or a feeling, of necessity. There was no feeling that it was a forever relationship, one that I couldn't live without. I've been sorry to see relationships end, but I've never felt devastated, or heartbroken."

"Don't you think it's odd that neither of us have been madly, passionately in love?"

"I think it's odder that people fall in and out of 'love' so easily. It makes me think it's not love, but infatuation."

"What do you even think love is?"

He shrugged. "I know familial love. Loyalty, respect, attachment, devotion."

"So, you love your family."

"I do, but that's an attachment formed over time." Brando shifted, faced her. "It's probably why I'm comfortable proposing marriage. I believe together we could raise our children with kindness and respect. We'll be devoted parents, and that devotion is binding…us to them, them to us, and for each other."

"That sounds dreadful. You know that, don't you? Every word you say just sounds dreadful."

"Dreadful, how? It's stability. It's honorable—"

"Devoid of passion, energy, excitement—"

"And yet, you yourself seem to avoid those very things," he interrupted.

She drew back. "What?"

"You deliberately avoid passion and excitement—"

"If that was true, I wouldn't be here, in this situation, now."

"And yet you've admitted more than once that our night together was a mistake."

She felt her face heat. "I don't do one-night stands," she said stiffly. "You were my first, and I realized belatedly that casual sex wasn't for me."

"*I* didn't blow you off, and it didn't have to be a one-night stand. I phoned you while you were on the way in the cab to the airport. I phoned you again after you landed in Los Angeles. You didn't return those two calls. Undeterred, I tried to see you again a couple weeks later, but you pushed me away, saying that while you'd enjoyed our night together, it wouldn't happen again."

"It couldn't, Brando. I've never mixed business and pleasure before. You were the first client I ever got…intimate…with."

"Why did you?"

"I liked you. I was drawn to you."

"And I liked you, and was very drawn to you, too."

"But I don't sleep with my clients," she said firmly. "It's bad business, and incredibly irresponsible of me."

"Don't work with the Ricci family anymore. Problem solved."

"It's not that easy, Brando. The Riccis are important clients. I can't alienate them."

"You can't alienate them, but you can alienate me?"

She sighed with frustration. "You're not helping, especially not when you twist my words. You know what I mean. I didn't have feelings for any of them… I had feelings for you, and that's a problem." And then realizing what she'd just said, she hurriedly added, "And now that I'm pregnant, we really have a problem. How do we raise this baby, and where?"

Brando was silent, his features shuttered, and then he rolled one thickly muscled shoulder. "Sometimes solutions come when you're not obsessing about them. Perhaps we need a break from talking and thinking. Perhaps we should go do something and just not think."

She arched a brow, curious. "Do what?"

"We could get in the car and drive to Greve, and then stop in Montefioralle, which is up on a hillside, and actually overlooks Greve. Montefioralle is a village that dates to the early nine hundreds and there are wonderful views of the valley from there. Many tourists like to walk to Montefioralle from Greve, but I wouldn't suggest it in your condition, but the drive is scenic and Greve has a charming, historic main square, and several nice spots we could stop for lunch."

Charlotte glanced at her laptop on the table and then out at the valley, and she knew what she wanted to do—escape. Not think. But being with Brando was incredibly problematic. "Can we really not discuss the baby and the future for the next hour?"

"I promise we won't discuss either for the rest of the afternoon. Let's leave serious discussions until later, and just try to enjoy the day. You're not in this part of Italy often. Try to enjoy it."

They drove to Greve in his low-slung sports car and parked in a small alley behind a creamy stone building, and then entered through the back of the building. It was cool inside, the thick stone walls keeping out the heat, while the interior smelled of oak and wine. "One of our tasting rooms," he said, guiding her past an office to the public rooms where he gave her a brief overview of the Ricci wines being sampled and sold in the shop.

After saying a few words to the staff, he escorted her through the front door, where they emerged onto the medieval town square, the square ringed with handsome buildings filled with picturesque cafés, art galleries and more wine tasting rooms. They wandered in and out of the different shops and galleries and visited a church where the stillness and flickering candles filled Charlotte with much-needed peace. Everything would be fine. She didn't have to panic or worry so much. Brando would be reasonable and they'd find a way through this.

After an hour and a half of exploring the town, they returned to Brando's car for the short drive up a steep hill to Montefioralle.

This time Brando parked at a small restaurant perched on the side of the slope with a breathtaking view of the valley and Greve below. "Hope you're hungry," he said as they were seated at a table on the small patio. "The food here is excellent, and the wine, too."

"Is it wine from your vineyard?" she asked.

He flashed a smile that was as sexy as it was sinful. "How did you know?"

She couldn't help smiling back. He was irresistible when he turned on the charm. "Just a lucky guess."

Brando had been intrigued by Charlotte from the first time he met her in August of last year. She was stylish, stunning, smart and incredibly confident. He was impressed she could hold her own during contentious meetings with his family, and admired her ability to say what needed to be said, even if it wasn't popular. Brando, himself, tended to be blunt, and it wasn't often he met a woman who'd go toe-to-toe with him, rather than shy away from tough topics, but she did. And then when the conflict eased, she'd smile one of her smiles, and maybe that's what had hooked him.

When Charlotte Parks smiled, she lit up a room. Her smile was brilliant and wide, and her blue eyes gleamed, too.

It wasn't until she smiled now that he realized this was the first time he'd seen her smile since their night together New Year's Eve.

He realized how much he'd missed that smile, never mind how much he'd flat out missed her.

Brando hadn't chased after a woman in years, but he'd wanted to see Charlotte last year, after she'd returned to the States. He'd very much wanted another night with her, although he suspected one more night wouldn't be enough for him. He'd gone to LA to see her, but she gave excuses about being busy, and in the middle of a tense situation with clients, but she hoped she could say hello the next time she was in Italy.

She was giving him the brush-off. He'd been equally surprised, and disappointed, because even though she'd said all along it would be one night only, he hadn't believed she meant it. But she had.

He admired that, too.

This wasn't a game for her, either. She truly valued her independence, and it was a refreshing change from the women he dated who were utterly dependent on him, craving attention, desiring to be spoiled, hungry for gifts, big and small. Brando knew he was as much at fault for cultivating shallow relationships. He preferred giving gifts over giving his heart. It was a tidier transaction. Fewer complications.

Only now the woman who didn't want him was here, pregnant with his child, and there would be no tidy transaction. Their situation was enormously complicated.

He leaned across the table and kissed her, a firm,

slow kiss. Her mouth was warm and soft and he felt the quiver in her lips before he drew back.

Her face was pale with two pink blotches in her cheekbones, which only made her blue eyes brighter. He could see the worry in her eyes, though, as well as a question. She didn't know why he'd kissed her. He didn't know, either, other than he wanted her. He'd wanted her from the very beginning, and it crossed his mind that he would probably always be this attracted to her, and not just physically, but intellectually. She held her own with him. She was his equal in every way. She'd make an excellent wife.

"You'll make an excellent addition to the family," he said. "If I didn't know better, I'd think you were a Ricci already."

Charlotte stiffened, her shoulders squaring, spine straightening. "We'd agreed we weren't going to discuss the future," she said quietly, flatly, anger washing through her. "Those were your words, too."

He gave a casual shrug. "I'm not discussing the future. I'm talking about the present. You fit in. You're my other half. You belong with me," he answered.

"I'm not your other half. You are a whole, and I am a whole and there is no room in our individual lives for each other. We are too independent, too headstrong."

“We’re smart enough, successful enough to know how to adjust.”

She held her breath, unwilling to speak, afraid that whatever she said might be used against her.

“What other choice do we have?” He’d ordered a glass of wine with his lunch and he gave his goblet a slight spin and watched the ruby-red wine swirl. “Not if we’re putting our child’s needs first, and I don’t know a lot about you, but I’ve heard enough now to understand that your family never put you first. That your fear of families is the fear of being lost, consumed—”

“That’s putting it a little strong,” she interrupted.

“But I’m right, aren’t I? You like your space because you can breathe, and be free, something you couldn’t do in your family.”

Suddenly parched, she reached for her water glass and took a gulp. “I might need a glass of wine, too, if we’re going to be analyzing me over lunch today.”

His lips lifted faintly. “No one is trying to psychoanalyze you. I’m just slowly starting to understand you. I think it’s important to understand you—”

“Then let me help you understand exactly what I don’t want. I don’t want to become part of another family. And as much as I enjoyed working with your family, I have no desire to become one of them. I mean no disrespect, and I apologize if I’m phrasing this badly, but your family is every bit as overwhelming as mine—and that doesn't work for me in any way."

"No need to apologize. I agree we are passionate, but there is no malice in any of them."

She didn't immediately reply. Instead she looked away, out across the restaurant's patio toward the verdant valley filled with orchards and vineyards. A vineyard ran down the hill below them, the afternoon sun shining brightly on the tidy rows of grapes, gilding the green leaves with burnished light.

"There's a reason I'm happy in Southern California," she said after a bit. "I'm on my own. I have my own place, my own identity. I don't have to answer to my mother, my father, or any of my stepparents. I can just be myself. It's taken me years to break free and I've no desire to give up that space, and independence."

"But isn't your mother still in Los Angeles?"

Charlotte shook her head. "This isn't something we discuss, but my mother and Bill have been separated for a couple of years. They may even be divorced by now. I don't know, and I don't really want to know. I figure when Mother wants to announce something she will, and until then I'm happy to leave her alone and let her do her thing, and I do my thing."

"Where is she living?"

"South of France at the moment, but I think that's a temporary thing."

"You don't see your stepfather anymore? I thought you two were once close?"

"I like Bill. He's a maverick and colorful and he always invites me to Hollywood parties, as well as his big film premieres. Sometimes I show up because he loves a good red carpet photo with his family all around him, but I haven't since he and Mom went their different ways. But I'm fine with it. I like Los Angeles because I can be no one there. I'm invisible and I like that. I also like the weather, I like being close to the ocean and I like that no one descends on me in Los Angeles. My father hates LA. My brothers and sisters hate LA, too, which delights me to no end. I'm happy with my little house and career. It suits me."

She felt him study her from across the table and it was all she could do to sit still beneath his scrutiny.

"Marrying me doesn't mean you'll lose your identity, *cara*. You will always be Charlotte Parks, even if you become Mrs. Charlotte Parks Ricci."

"What if I didn't want to take your last name? What if I simply wanted to be Charlotte Parks?"

His powerful shoulders shifted easily. "If that is what you preferred, I'd have no objections. You have a career, you have a perfectly lovely name. Marrying you is about giving our baby a home, a family and a family name." He paused. "Or do you take issue with our baby being named Ricci?"

She couldn't believe she was even having this

conversation. She wasn't seriously considering marrying him, was she?

She sat silent for a moment, processing everything being said, and realizing she maybe had given an indication that she was open to marrying him… But was she?

Was she even considering this future he suggested?

As if able to read her mind, he added, "It's not as if I live in my family's back pocket. There are family business meetings, as well as periodic family dinners, holidays and birthday celebrations, but my brothers and sister are busy with their own lives and families. They certainly wouldn't be overly involved in our lives, nor would we be expected to be immersed in theirs, not as newlyweds with a young baby."

"You realize I haven't agreed to marry you, nor is it likely that I will accept your proposal," she said.

"Yes, that's understood," he answered gravely, and yet she could have sworn his lips twitched, as if amused. "So, let's just keep moving forward, and discussing options, aware that no commitments are being made, on either side."

"Fair enough," she said before looking him in the eyes. "How important is it for the baby to take your last name? Would it upset your family terribly?"

His jaw flexed, and he frowned into his wineglass. "I don't know if it would bother them. It would bother me. I'd very much like my son or daughter to have my name."

"I thought you were the rebel."

"I've been a rebel, but I'm older, and wiser, and appreciate my family, and our history here in Tuscany. Riccis have been making wine for one hundred years—"

"But you're the only one still making wine. The others have all shifted to other industries."

"All the more reason for me to want a son or daughter to carry on the winemaking tradition."

She didn't immediately reply, because there was nothing she could say. She understood him, and if she were in his position, she'd feel the same way. It was only later, as they drove back to his *castello*, and passed through the huge gates set in the high stone walls that she said quietly, "We don't have to be married for our child to take your name. You are the father. The birth certificate will reflect your name."

He glanced at her, lips compressing, but that was his only response as they traveled down the private lane lined with tall cypresses.

Brando parked in front of the *castello*, turned the ignition off and faced her. "Do you still intend to go to London tomorrow?"

"Yes."

"I'll fly you there. It'll be easier on you physically. You won't have to deal with long lines and security."

His offer caught her off guard, and yet at the same time, it was a little bit tempting. All London airports were unbearable. You couldn't escape the crowds and lines. But why would he want to fly her back to England? "I'm not sure how flying me to England benefits you."

"Less stress on you is less stress on the baby."

Ah, of course. It was about the baby. She didn't know why she felt a stab of disappointment, but she certainly wasn't going to analyze the reaction here and now. "And there is no other agenda?" she asked, arching a brow. "You're not planning on announcing we're engaged, or something outrageous like that?"

He matched her arched brow with one of his. "How can I do that, when we're not engaged? Really, Charlotte, you have so little trust."

His smirk was galling. But then everything about him was frustrating. He was gorgeous and interesting and he made her feel alive and wistful and confused…

She hated feeling confused. As well as wistful. Both reminded her of being a child, which wasn't a period in her life she remembered with fondness. Being a child, she was forced to rely on others, and the chief lesson from her childhood seemed to be that people weren't dependable, that most promises made were never kept. "I don't trust people very much, no."

"You ought to begin trying to trust me, especially if we're to co-parent."

"I haven't agreed to that, either."

"*Bella*, fortunately for me, that one is out of your jurisdiction. The law gives us both rights as parents. However, if you feel like agreeing to something, you could agree to marry me so when I do meet your family tomorrow, I can be introduced as your fiancé, and the father of your baby."

"Maybe I should simply take my flight as scheduled. It would be far less complicated."

"Or, I fly you home and meet your family and you can introduce me as the father of your child. I think it would be reassuring for them to know you haven't been abandoned and won't be having to raise the child on your own."

For a split second she couldn't breathe, her chest squeezing, her heart suffused with pain. *That she hadn't been abandoned.* She blinked hard, clearing the hot sting of tears, trying to suppress the emotions that were threatening to swallow her whole.

"Surely your father would be reassured by the news," Brando added, brow creasing. "As well as your brothers and sisters."

"Everyone is quite busy," she said, forcing a smile. "I don't think my pregnancy will trouble them one way or another, but you suddenly appearing with me would cause a fuss. And we don't need the fuss, do we?"

He gave her a long, considering look. "What happens when the gossips discover you're pregnant with my child? That will get lots of tabloid attention, but if that doesn't worry you…?"

"We'll deal with it when we have to. Hopefully it won't be for quite some time."

CHAPTER SIX

CHARLOTTE WOKE SEVERAL times in the night, not feeling well. Her lower back ached. Her lower belly felt heavy and tight. She'd leave bed and walk a bit, and then stretch and eventually she'd fall back asleep.

But the heaviness in her lower back was far worse this morning, and the tightness in her lower belly had become a perplexing cramp. The cramping sensation had become strong, and regular, far too regular. She'd read about Braxton Hicks contractions and wondered if this was what she was experiencing. She even looked them up online, but these didn't quite meet the description. No, hers felt strong, and the dull pain was intensifying to the point she couldn't walk easily anymore.

Something wasn't right.

The cramping was frightening, and the pain was becoming excruciating.

Charlotte had left her cell phone unplugged during the night after researching contractions, and now it was dead, the battery dying in the night.

Limping to the door, she prayed she'd spot one of the staff nearby. Fortunately, one of the maids was walking down the hall with a stack of freshly laundered towels.

"I need Brando," Charlotte said in Italian, panting and wincing as another sharp contraction hit. "Tell him something's wrong. I think the baby is coming."

"You must lie down," the maid answered. "Let me help you to bed, and then I'll send for help."

Brando was there at her side in less than five minutes. He was wearing jeans, work boots and a thin knit shirt, indicating that he'd been out in the fields again this morning. He leaned over her, his gaze searching hers. "What's happening?"

"Strong contractions. It doesn't feel right."

"You think the baby is coming?"

"I don't know, but I'm scared. It's too soon."

He reached for her hand and gave it a reassuring squeeze. "I've sent for my pilot. He should be here soon. He'll get us to the hospital quickly."

"What if there's something wrong? What if the baby—?"

He gave her hand another warm, firm squeeze. "We're only thinking positive thoughts, *cara.* Be positive, be strong."

Brando stayed with her until the pilot texted that he was on premises and the helicopter was ready. There was a small hospital in the valley that served the local population, but Brando was taking no chances. They were going to go to Florence where there were specialists and a neonatal unit, just in case one was needed.

The moment the pilot indicated they were good to go, Brando scooped Charlotte into his arms and carried her downstairs to the helipad, feeling her contractions as they hit, and soothing her when she expressed pain, and then fear and alarm. “It is all good, all fine,” he said, looking into her eyes, letting her see his calm, and confidence.

“Can the baby survive at six months? I think so, but I’m not sure.”

“This baby is fierce, and strong, it wanted to be conceived, so yes, I think this baby can survive. Absolutely.”

She smiled even as she blinked back tears. “It is a stubborn little thing.”

“Maybe because its mother is stubborn, too.”

She smiled a little bigger, the smile still wobbly, but he found it hopelessly endearing. “And you’re not?”

“I’m the most reasonable, rational man you’ll ever meet.”

“You forgot arrogant. As long as the baby’s okay—” She broke off, eyes filling with tears.

“The baby will be fine. And you will be fine.”

“And if something goes wrong?”

“If there are complications, you will know you are being seen by the best doctors, at one of the best hospitals in Europe, and I will be with you every step of the way. Have faith. Trust me."

"I'm trying." She gripped his hand tightly, desperately, as she searched his face. After a moment, she added brokenly, "I want this baby."

"I do, too."

The helicopter had them arrive in Florence in less than twenty minutes, and they were greeted immediately by a medical team.

As he'd promised, Brando stayed by Charlotte's side during the examination. He held his breath as the obstetrician checked her, and then performed an ultrasound. Thankfully, the baby's heartbeat was steady, and the baby looked fine.

Brando stared at the screen, taking in every detail. He hadn't seen many ultrasounds before, but unless his eyes were deceiving him, that was most definitely a boy baby.

His chest tightened and his throat ached with overwhelming emotion.

Charlotte was pregnant with his son.

"He's really okay?" Brando asked quietly.

Charlotte looked from the doctor to Brando and back to the physician. "It's a boy?"

The doctor nodded. "Yes, and your son looks good. He is fine. But you, Charlotte, are in preterm labor. We're going to try to stop labor, as the best place for your son is right where he is now, safe inside his mother."

"Can you stop the labor?" she asked.

The doctor didn't even hesitate. "Because you sought out treatment immediately, I think we have a good shot at it."

It was a long day, but by midafternoon the contractions had stopped, and finally pain free, Charlotte fell asleep, worn out from the worry and fear. Brando stood by her bed in her private room on the hospital's maternity ward, watching her sleep.

Her color was better than it had been this morning. Her long blond hair spilled across her pillow, her lips slightly parted in sleep.

The tension was gone from her face, and he felt as if he could breathe properly for the first time all day.

He'd been scared, truly scared, and he'd prayed not just for the baby, but for Charlotte, who seemed so determined to be an island and do everything, and manage everything, on her own. He'd seen her panic, and felt her fear, and for the first time, he saw a crack in that perfect, flawless mask of hers. She might not want anyone else to know, but she felt vulnerable, as well as alone, which perplexed him, as she came from a big family and yet it was a family she didn't seem to embrace.

His phone vibrated with incoming messages and he drew his phone from his pocket, scanned the texts and then checked his emails, and seeing nothing that required immediate attention, he pulled a chair closer to the side of the bed and sat down.

When he told her he would be there, with her, he'd meant it.

Charlotte and his son might be out of danger, but there was nowhere Brando wanted to be but here, with her. With them. His family.

His family, he silently repeated, mulling the words over, awed by the implication. He was going to have a son.

Warmth filled him and his chest felt tight with inarticulate emotion. Pride, hope, wonder.

Growing up in a close, overly involved family had made him at times resent the family ties, and then during his early twenties, he'd had a falling-out with his family, particularly his father, whom Brando viewed as overbearing and interfering.

It didn't help that Brando did not feel wanted, or needed, by the family, and questioned why every family member was expected to go to work for the Ricci-Baldi company. He already had two older brothers and a sister working in the business, and they were content. Why was he needed? He wasn't. And the work he was being offered was menial at best. He found every aspect of working for the family to be boring and mindless—tasks anyone could handle. After a year of miserably working for the family, he realized he could go do this same pointless brainless work somewhere else and be paid a hell of a lot better than what he was earning working for his family.

He spoke to his father about his boredom, and

his father dismissed Brando's concerns, stating that everyone was expected to prove themselves, and that as the youngest, he couldn't expect to ever be in a leadership position, not when Enzo and Marcello were already working their way up through management.

His father's answer didn't sit well with Brando, and in an act of utter rebellion, he returned the call from a modeling agency in Milan, and said he'd be open to meeting with the agency if they were still interested in him. During his teenage years, Brando had been approached several times about modeling, but he knew it wasn't something that would be viewed favorably in his family, so he'd turned the opportunities down. But now, in need of work, he went on his first go-see, booked the job and proceeded to book almost every other go-see he was sent out on.

Brando's father did exactly as expected—Brando was cut off from the family financially, but Brando wasn't upset. He was relieved. For the first time in his life, he was standing completely on his own and being successful. In six months, he made more money than he had in the previous two years, and by the time he turned twenty-five he was making so much money he needed to find investment opportunities, reluctant to leave that much cash sitting in the bank. He bought stocks, and purchased real estate, and when those proved to be good investments, he became a venture capitalist for two small technology start-ups, turning his hundreds of thousands into millions when one of the start-ups went public and became big.

At twenty-six he bought his first small winery. Within two years he'd bought another, and it was at this time his father came to him and asked if he'd come back to the family and work with them since Brando seemed to have a golden touch. Brando was still trying to decide if he would when his father died, and if Brando had one regret it was that his father died before Brando returned to the family, going to work in Florence with his brothers and sister, refocusing the Ricci brands and giving new life to the Ricci wines.

His mother used to say that she was sure Brando's father knew, but maybe it wasn't important that his father knew. Maybe what was important was that those living knew Brando would never shirk his responsibilities, or his familial duty, again.

Family came first, always.

Charlotte woke to the sound of murmured voices and, opening her eyes, discovered Brando at the foot of her bed in discussion with her doctor.

Brando was the one to notice she'd awoken and he immediately approached the bed, a question in his silver gaze. "How do you feel?"

"Better," she said, grateful the contractions had stopped, and there was no more pain. "What time is it?"

“Close to seven. Your doctor was just doing a final check on you before going home for the night.”

She glanced over at the doctor as he approached her side. “Thank you for all your help today.”

“My pleasure. I’m just glad you could get here quickly. Everything looks good right now,” he answered, adding, “You’ll be in excellent hands here tonight, and the staff knows I’m on call should you need anything.”

Brando walked the doctor out before returning. “Are you hungry? You haven’t had breakfast or lunch.”

“I am starting to get hungry.”

“Good, my personal chef is on the way now with dinner. When he heard we were back in town, he said there was no way we could eat hospital food. He’s been cooking all afternoon, and I see you looking worried, but there’s no reason for that. I’ve cleared the menu with the doctor, and the doctor said soup, pasta and a little bit of meat would help keep up your strength.”

“You’ve thought of everything.”

“I don’t want you to stress. You’re to relax, and eat dinner, and sleep well tonight, and tomorrow we’ll see what the doctor says. Hopefully you won’t have to stay here too long.”

It was only then that Charlotte remembered her flight. “I missed it. My flight to London.”

“Thank goodness you weren’t in-flight. I don’t

think today's outcome would have been the same if you were on the plane."

"No, I don't think so, either." She slowly exhaled, trying to ease the tension in her chest. "I came close to going into labor."

"*Cara*, you were in labor. The doctors were able to administer medicine to stop it. But another thirty minutes… I don't know the outcome. We might have had our son with us tonight."

"I'm only twenty-three weeks along. I don't think the odds would be very good for him."

"I learned today that half of the babies born between twenty-three and twenty-four weeks survive delivery and have a shot at life outside the neonatal ICU."

"But that doesn't include all the complications premature babies have, does it?"

"No." His expression sobered, and he reached out to smooth hair back from her brow, his touch unexpectedly tender. "Which is why you need to rest and relax and give our son as much time as possible."

She watched the door after he walked out, apparently to make a call, or whatever it was he'd said, feeling raw and shaken. Not just from today's early labor scare, but from his kindness, and his strength, and his calm in the middle of a storm. She always tried to be calm during dramas, but she always felt like a fraud, not truly calm, not truly collected. It was an image she projected, aware that the world preferred strength, and people were drawn to success, but sometimes being strong and successful was isolating.

Sometimes being the one who had it together and needed nothing from anyone meant you had very little support from others.

Perhaps if she'd learned to ask for help, or was comfortable demanding attention, she might feel less alone. Perhaps if she was better at trusting people, she might have had proper relationships... Maybe she'd even be romantically involved with someone.

Instead she admired interesting men from afar, careful to never get too involved, careful to never risk her heart.

At least, until she gave in to her impulse and spent a night with Brando, and that night changed everything—and she wasn't referencing the pregnancy, but her hopes, and dreams.

She cared for Brando...a lot.

She also knew it was incredibly unrealistic to think he might have genuine feelings for her. He'd proposed because he was old-fashioned, and in his mind it was the morally right thing to do. She knew he would marry her, too, for the very same reasons. But he didn't love her, and she doubted he could be faithful, but she couldn't marry someone who didn't want her, not truly want her.

Brando returned to the room just then, entering with a man in a sharp suit, and the only indication that he might be Brando's chef was that he carried a large hamper in one hand, and an oversize insulated carrier in the other. The chef went to work spreading a small cloth over her table and laying out dishes, and Charlotte keep her attention fixed on the chef so that she didn't look at Brando even though she was incredibly aware of him, and that he was watching her.

No one had ever watched her the way he watched her.

No one had ever paid her as much attention or listened to her when she asked for space. He'd even let her go last winter when she wanted that, too.

Charlotte had met many powerful men, and a few handsome, powerful men, but she'd never met anyone who respected her desires the way Brando did. He could have tried to steamroll over her, but instead he appealed to her intellect and reason, and for that, she was grateful.

The chef was then gone as quickly as he'd arrived. Brando served her and then himself, and they ate the delicate seafood risotto, and while Brando had some of the main course of meat, Charlotte was satisfied.

She watched him as he cleared the dinner dishes, filling the basket before refreshing her water from the large bottle of sparkling water the chef had brought with him. "Thank you," she said, a lump in her throat because honestly, she couldn't remember the last time someone had done so much for her, never mind waiting on her hand and foot.

"My pleasure," he answered. "You do remember there is dessert. Mousse *al cioccolato.* Your favorite."

Chocolate mousse. It was her favorite, and he'd remembered.

They'd had chocolate mousse the night she'd stayed over, and she'd straddled him in bed, feeding him spoonfuls, before deciding it was far too good to share. She blushed, heat rushing through her. "Was this just a lucky coincidence, or did you ask him to make it?"

"I asked him."

Charlotte was dangerously close to tears. She clutched the covers in her hands, holding them tightly. "I'm overwhelmed."

"By mousse?"

"No, by you, today." She felt the hard thudding of her heart, and the strange prickly emotion in her chest, emotion that seemed to zigzag all the way through her. She hadn't been a virgin when she met Brando, and yet he made her feel naive, untutored, inexperienced in the ways of the world. He made her want to believe that better things existed, and that people could be good, and patient, and kind.

Today Brando also made her aware of just how much she needed him, even if she didn't want to admit it.

She didn't know what would have happened if she hadn't been with him when the contractions began. She didn't know how she would have managed without him today. He'd handled everything, and he'd been so incredibly focused, and calm, and strong. He'd said he wouldn't let anything happen to her, and he'd meant it. He'd been incredibly proactive, as well as protective. It was rather humbling to realize how good it felt to let someone else take charge. To let someone else be strong.

"Have I thanked you for today?" she said. "I don't know how I—"

"You have thanked me," he interrupted quietly. "But you don't have to thank me. I wanted to be here. There is nowhere else I'd rather be."

She gave a half nod. "I believe you."

The corner of his mouth lifted a fraction. "Are we making progress, *cara*?"

"I don't know if I'd call it progress, but you should know I appreciate everything, and am grateful, and our baby is grateful, too." And for the first time, the words *our baby* felt right. They felt true. It was their baby and there would be no shutting Brando out, and no fighting over custody. How could she do that to him? He would be a wonderful father, and she couldn't deny him the opportunity to be there every step of the way, or their son the security of a devoted father, either.

Brando misread her contemplative mood as fatigue, and insisted he leave for the night so she could get some sleep. "The nurse knows to call me if you want anything, or if you suddenly crave gelato, or if you're wide awake in the middle of the night and just want to talk."

She smiled crookedly. "I can call you just to chat?"

"If you're lonely or bored, have the nurse call me, and I will keep you company on the other end of the line."

"And if I wanted you to come back and keep me company here?" she asked.

"I'd get dressed and come straight away."

"What if I wanted you to stay here with me tonight?" The words popped out before she'd thought them through.

"Do you want me to? I've been told the little couch makes into a bed."

She eyed the small couch and then looked at him. He was over six feet two, and his shoulders were wider than the sleek Italian sofa. "You wouldn't be comfortable."

"I don't mind, not if it'd give you peace of mind."

She tried to picture him sleeping so close to her, his big body sprawled out, just the way he'd slept with her during their night together when they'd finally stopped touching and kissing and tasting—

"No, I wouldn't sleep a wink," she answered. "Go home and come back tomorrow…if you have time."

"*Cara*, I have nothing but time." He leaned over the bed, kissed her brow and then a fleeting kiss on her lips. "Can I get you anything before I leave?"

And suddenly, just like that, she didn't want him to leave.

Not just now, but ever.

The simmering feelings she'd had for him six months ago had become a fireball, exploding to life.

"No," she said, hating the thickness in her throat, and the aching pang in her heart. "I'm good. Go home, sleep well. I'll see you tomorrow."

Easier said than done, Brando thought, back at his elegant town house in the converted palace. He wandered through the second floor and then up to the third floor, which was his private office suite. Sitting down at his desk, he sorted through mail that had been left for him by his assistant, and documents requiring signatures. He signed where necessary and then leaned back and stared across the room, to the summer sky just now going dark.

He thought of nothing and everything, of Charlotte in the hospital bed, and the ultrasound earlier where he saw his son for the first time, the baby so tiny, but also so very perfect. Brando knew he would do whatever he had to do to ensure his son's safety, as well as his future. What mattered now was Charlotte and the baby. Everything else was secondary.

His phone pinged with an incoming text. He looked at it immediately, in case it had to do with Charlotte. Instead it was a text from Louisa.

Hello, handsome. I'm free now. Are you?

Brando picked up the phone and texted back.

Sorry, no.

He thought for a moment, before sending another swift text.

I enjoyed our time together, but I am no longer single. Ciao e abbi cura di te.

Goodbye and take care.

CHAPTER SEVEN

BRANDO WAS BACK at the hospital in the morning and Charlotte was sitting up in bed, looking anxious and restless when he arrived. "What's wrong?" he asked, leaning over to greet her with a kiss on her forehead.

"I need my phone, and my computer. I can't work without them." She gestured to the short stack of magazines on the bedside table. "The nurse brought me fashion magazines this morning but I don't want to read them. I need to check in with my clients—"

"Easy, slow down," he said, checking his smile as he pulled a chair close to the side of the bed. "You're supposed to be resting, not stressing out."

Charlotte drew a deep breath. "I know, and I agree. But I feel naked without my phone, and it's even worse not having a phone or computer. I'm not used to being completely out of touch."

"Do you want me to have someone drive them up from the *castello*? I can."

Her brow furrowed. "Am I going to be here long?"

"I don't know. That's something we'll have to ask the doctor when he makes his rounds this morning."

She was silent a moment and then nodded. "Obviously if me being here is the best thing, then I should be here. I just would feel better being here if I had my vanity bag, and briefcase with laptop, phone and chargers."

"I'm worried work will create stress for you, though."

"I'd be more stressed not being able to communicate with my clients." She hesitated. "I'll let them know I'm taking the next week or two off and will be in touch soon. I'd feel better about that than just not answering emails."

"Agreed."

She looked at him, brows still knitting together, expression still troubled. "I'm not flying anytime soon, am I?"

"I think it would be incredibly risky."

"I do, too." She looked past him to the window with its view of the city and the hills that framed the capital of Tuscany. "I don't want a repeat of yesterday."

"Neither do I."

"I was terrified."

He saw her bring her hands together, fingers laced tightly against the white hospital covers, and he reached out and covered her clenched hands with one of his. "Everything is good," he said quietly, firmly, determined to keep her calm. Relaxed. The baby needed her to be still, and relaxed.

"For now," she said, a catch in her voice. She glanced up at him, blue eyes shining with a film of tears. "But I can't stop thinking about the what-ifs. What if I'd been on the plane? What if I'd been going through customs at the airport? What if—?"

"But you weren't. You were with me, and we got you here quickly and the doctors were able to stop labor." He squeezed her hands. "And it wasn't all bad. Yesterday we saw the baby and he's healthy, and beautiful—"

She snorted. "I wouldn't go so far as to describe him as beautiful. I'm sure he will be—"

"He was beautiful to me. My son. *Our* son." Brando's voice deepened. "It's a miracle. I wasn't expecting a family and yet suddenly I have one, and I vow to take care of you both, always. Forever."

He hoped his words would reassure her, but instead tears trembled on her lashes before falling.

She pulled her hands free to wipe them away. "I hate crying," she said hoarsely. "Please don't mind me."

His chest squeezed, and he felt a peculiar pang near his heart. "You don't have to be an island," he said carefully, not wanting to upset her. "It's okay to have feelings and cry. Italian women are passionate, and emotional, but those emotions do not make them weak. Emotions are what make us strong."

She swiped beneath her eyes, drying them. "You seem to understand women quite well."

"Somehow you manage to make that sound like a criticism."

"In so many ways you seem so perfect, but then you don't want serious relationships. You aren't married—"

"If I was married, we wouldn't be here today. I would have never had that night with you."

She gazed up at him from beneath wet spiky lashes. "Lots of men have affairs."

"Are you thinking of that survey from a number of years ago that said in Italy, most affairs started in the office?"

"No, but interesting." Two bright spots of pink colored her cheeks. "I just know my parents divorced over affairs, and it was a problem between my mom and her last husband."

"I don't condone affairs. And I don't know if my father ever had an affair, but he cherished my mother, and taught his sons to protect your family at all costs, and you can't protect your family if you're damaging the marriage."

"So when you marry, you won't have one?"

"It goes against everything I believe."

"Then why haven't you married?"

"Because I hadn't found the one I wanted to commit myself to for the rest of time."

Charlotte's heart fell, and she looked away, teeth catching her lower lip to keep it from quivering.

Brando would marry her because it was the right thing to do, but she wasn't the one he would have married. And yet yesterday had made her realize she couldn't manage everything by herself. She'd been prepared to go it alone when she'd felt good and strong, but if there were complications, or if the baby came early, she realized she wouldn't be able to cope on her own. She didn't want to struggle alone.

"Remember when we agreed we'd be honest?" she said, stomach in knots, pulse racing.

He nodded.

"I'm going to be honest with you now, but it's not easy because I like my independence, but it's a problem." She glanced at him, trying to read his expression, but his silver gaze hid whatever he was thinking. "I was wrong. I can't do this on my own." She drew a quick breath and plunged on. "I can't even imagine what I would have done if I were in California when this happened. I don't know what I would have done yesterday without you. I was so scared, and in so much pain." She pressed her lips together, and counted a few counts, giving her time to gain control over her emotions, not easy when her heart felt bruised and she felt overwhelmed by the reality of her situation. "I try so hard to be independent and handle things, but Brando, I've never been so scared in my life. It was too soon for the baby to come, and I just kept thinking of all the problems he'd have if he was born at almost twenty-four weeks."

"It *was* scary, but you're fine, and he's fine—"

"For now." She looked up into his face, her gaze meeting his, and holding. This was serious. Important. She needed him to realize just how serious she was now. "But what if I go into labor again? What if the baby is born early? He could have serious challenges—" She broke off, swallowed and continued. "I was naive to think I could do it all, handle it all on my own. Honestly, it wasn't just naive, it was selfish. He isn't just my baby, he's yours, too, and you need to be part of his life."

"I will be."

She nodded, again biting down into her tender lower lip. For a moment there was just silence and then she added softly, "You were wonderful yesterday. You were such an advocate and so calm and so strong—" She broke off, fighting to hold back fresh tears, uncertain as to why she was falling apart now. She didn't cry and yet she felt as if she were a watering pot, tears springing free. "I realized I can't do this without you. I don't want to do this without you—"

The rest of Charlotte's thought was interrupted by the sudden appearance of the doctor with a nurse, and they entered her room in the middle of conversation, but the conversation ended as the obstetrician approached the bed.

"How are we today?" Dr. Leonardi asked, glancing from Charlotte to Brando and back again. "I understand it was a restless night for our patient. The night nurse said you were awake much of the night, but we need you to rest."

Brando looked at Charlotte, a black eyebrow lifting. She ignored it, and him, and answered the doctor. "I didn't realize hospitals are so noisy, and every time the nurse came in to check on me I'd wake up and then stay awake." She realized how that sounded and quickly added, "I'm not complaining, I'm just explaining why I couldn't sleep."

"You couldn't pretend it was a fine hotel?" the doctor teased.

"If it was a hotel, I would have phoned the front desk and complained," she answered with a wry smile. "I think I just had too much time on my own, and no way to distract myself. Brando has promised to send for my computer and then I'll be able to work if I can't sleep."

"Is your work very taxing?" Dr. Leonardi asked. "We don't want you to do anything that will create stress. It might be better for you to read a relaxing book, nothing too scary or violent. Maybe a romance. My wife reads them and says they're very good for escaping."

Charlotte forced a pleasant expression, hiding how she truly felt, as she would never, ever be caught reading a romance. A biography, yes. A history, yes. A cozy mystery, yes. Romances were for those who believed in happy endings. She didn't, at least, not anymore.

"Do you have an idea of how long you'll want to keep her here?" Brando asked.

"Another day or two, and then we can evaluate how she's doing, and how the baby is doing. If both are doing well, I don't see why Charlotte couldn't go home with you, but I'd keep her on modified bed rest."

Charlotte's heart fell. "For how long?"

"Possibly for the duration of your pregnancy."

Her jaw dropped. Three months?

Brando crossed his arms over his chest. "What is modified bed rest?"

"It's a term we use for restricted activity without the stringent dictate to remain completely confined to bed. Every doctor probably has his own definition for it. For me it means limited physical activity, and lengthy morning and afternoon rest periods in bed. I also restrict lovemaking, so no sexual activity, as sex releases prostaglandins that are similar to the medications used to induce labor."

Charlotte blushed. "That won't be an issue," she said unsteadily. "We're not having sex."

"It won't be forever," the doctor replied with a smile. "After the baby you'll need a few weeks to heal, and then you should be able to resume sexual intercourse—"

"Any other concerns?" Charlotte interrupted,

embarrassed, and more than a little horrified. "Or do I just stay put for the day?"

"Just stay put, and relax, and I'll be back later this afternoon." The doctor nodded, smiled and walked out with the nurse.

Charlotte couldn't even look at Brando. Everything was so strange, and so uncomfortable. Her life seemed to be spinning completely out of control. "So there's that," she said, plucking at her covers.

"No sex for us—"

"That's not what I'm talking about," she interrupted quickly, heat rushing through her, making her feel tingly and self-conscious. "And you know it. You're just tormenting me now."

"Sex is what got us into this situation," he said mildly. "And it was good sex. Probably the best sex I've ever had."

She jerked her head up as she looked across her room at him. He was leaning against the wall, one shoulder resting against the window trim, sunlight pouring in, haloing his head with golden light. He had a hint of a smile, and there was a glint in his silver eyes that made her tummy flip and her pulse quicken. He was tall and lean, and incredibly handsome.

And he was hers…or had been for one night.

Two days ago he suggested they marry, which meant he could be hers forever.

Would he be happy, though? Would she?

"We were talking about something important

when Dr. Leonardi walked in," he said now, his smile disappearing, his expression turning serious. "Let's finish that conversation."

"I don't remember what we were saying—"

"You'd just said you couldn't do this alone, and you didn't want to." Brando repeated her words back to her, almost exactly as she'd said them. "So what do we do?" he added. "What is our next step?"

Her mouth dried and her pulse jumped, beating too hard in her veins. "You tell me."

"I want to hear it from you. We both already know what I think."

She swallowed hard, her mouth feeling as if she'd been sucking on a cotton ball. It took forever to form words, but Brando waited, saying nothing, just watching her with those piercing eyes of his. "You think...you believe...you said, we should...marry."

"And what do you think?" he said bluntly.

She felt another sharp twinge in her chest. "I think we do what's best for the baby."

"Which is?"

He wasn't making this easy, was he? She drew a deep breath, feeling tender and shy. "We get married."

"When?"

Her shoulders rose and fell. "Whenever we can?"

Brando needed to head to the Ricci headquarters for a meeting that couldn't be postponed, but he promised to be back for a late lunch. He returned two and a half hours later with lunch and her briefcase and her vanity bag. She didn't know if she was more excited at being able to brush her hair or check her email.

Again Brando's chef materialized with lunch, and after lunch was cleaned up and put away, Brando opened his laptop and worked, while she worked on hers. She handled the most urgent emails, and then sent emails to others letting them know that she was taking the next few weeks off for a personal matter, but hoped to be working again by the end of the month.

It wasn't until she got a flurry of email responses from her clients asking if everything was all right that she realized her wording was problematic. Normally Charlotte was an expert at handling sensitive matters but she certainly wasn't handling her own situation very well.

She didn't realize she'd muttered any of her frustration out loud until Brando asked what the matter was.

She sighed and rubbed at her temple, trying to make the headache go away. "I think I've made a mess of things," she said. "I reached out to my clients and let them know I'd be taking some time off, and it's backfired. Everyone is asking if I'm okay, and if there is anything they can do." She grimaced. "Someone just now wanted to know how they could help. This is exactly what I didn't want to happen."

"Read what you wrote."

"I said I was taking the next few weeks off for a

personal matter, but hoped to be back at work by the end of June." She looked over at him. "I shouldn't have said 'personal matter,' should've I?"

"You could have said 'wedding and honeymoon' and everyone would have been delighted, instead of worried." He saw her expression and shrugged. "It's the perception of things, isn't it? One sounds as if you're in the midst of struggle and sorrow, whereas 'wedding and honeymoon' sounds festive and celebratory."

"I can't tell my clients I'm getting married!"

"Why not? You are. Why not let them be happy for you?"

"But we don't know when we'll get married. It might not be for months."

"*Cara*, we're marrying soon. I'm determined we marry before our son is born, and since he seems to want to arrive early, I don't think we should wait."

She closed her laptop and pressed it to her chest. "How soon?"

"As soon as it can be arranged."

Brando was still with her when Dr. Leonardi returned late afternoon to check on Charlotte but stepped out while the doctor examined her, returning when it was over.

"Everything still looks good. I think she's out of the woods, but I want her on bed rest for the next few days, and then modified bed rest Friday."

Charlotte glanced hopefully at Brando. "Does that mean I can leave?"

"Perhaps tomorrow."

"But if everything looks good, can't I just rest at home?" she pressed.

Brando's gaze swept the sterile room. "I'd prefer for her to rest at my home. I'm not a fan of hospitals, and Charlotte is right, it's not very restful here. It's noisy and chaotic and I'm not sure how this is the best environment for her, or the baby."

"But we have nurses here, staff here. Equipment here," the doctor answered.

"Can't I get the same equipment for the house? Couldn't I hire a nurse to be with her at home?"

"That's a huge expense—" The doctor broke off when he saw Brando's expression. "But yes, she could be monitored at home. It's essential, though, that she rest, or you'll be right back here, and I don't know if we would be successful stopping labor next time."

"We have no intention of being back until the baby is full term," Brandon said.

Dr. Leonardi nodded. "I'll sign off on her leaving tomorrow. I still want her here tonight, but remember, no stress, no excitement. There isn't to be any drama or pressure."

"Understood."

Charlotte had imagined they'd be going to Brando's city house when she was discharged the next day.

Instead the helicopter was waiting to whisk them back to the *castello.*

"There is more fresh air, more peace in the country," Brando said as they made the fifteen-minute trip by air.

Now that she wasn't in pain, Charlotte enjoyed the trip, thinking the Tuscan hills looked like a striking quilt from the air, patches of light green and dark green intermixed with squares of pale gold, which turned out to be villages and *castellos* like Brando's.

On landing at his estate, Brando swept her into his arms and carried her back to the house, despite Charlotte insisting she could walk partway. He ignored her completely, and made short work of the distance, carrying her up two flights of stairs as if she weighed nothing at all.

She'd wondered about the third flight of stairs, and it wasn't until they reached a different bedroom that she realized Brando wasn't returning her to the bedroom she'd had before, but moving her into his room. "What are you doing?" she asked lowly as she was settled onto the enormous bed.

"Keeping you close," he said. "Doctor's orders."

"I thought you were getting a professional."

"I am, for the day. But at night, you'll sleep with me so I can keep an eye on you."

"And you don't think that will be a source of stress or excitement?"

"I think it will be a greater source of stress and

excitement if I come check on you three or four times a night."

She pulled herself up, sitting a little taller. "You don't need to do that. I can just shout."

"Right." But his lips twisted. He'd caught her attempt at humor.

She appreciated that, and him. More than he'd ever know. "I don't know that I can sleep in here with you."

"Why not?"

"I don't sleep well with others."

"Build a pillow wall."

"Can I really?"

"No. I need to be able to see you—"

"Nothing is going to happen! I'm not going to disappear in the night or give birth in ten seconds. Everything is fine. I just need to stay put—"

"In my bed."

"Brando, you're causing me stress and excitement."

"*Bella*, you're causing stress and excitement by arguing with me. Accept the inevitable. You're stuck with me." And then he closed the distance, bent down and kissed her, in a long, tender, melting kiss that made the hair rise on the back of her neck and her nipples peak and tighten. By the time he lifted his head, she felt like he'd poured warm honey into her veins. "It won't be all bad, though," he murmured, his lips brushing across hers in another slow, maddening kiss that had her squirming and breathless. "You just have to relax," he murmured, kissing her cheek and then just beneath her earlobe. He'd found an incredibly sensitive spot there, and then another one just beneath her jaw.

She sighed, and arched, pleasure suffusing her. "I'm not sure the doctor would approve," she whispered.

"I promise not to give you an orgasm."

She laughed softly, and the husky laugh turned to a smothered moan as his teeth scraped the side of her neck, setting her on fire, and sending hot sparks all the way down to her toes. She reached for him then, her hand wrapping around his nape as she buried her fingers into his thick, crisp hair. "If your kisses send me back to the hospital, I will—"

"Never forgive myself," he answered, lifting his head, to gaze down into her eyes. He pushed back a heavy wave of her hair, tucking strands behind her ear. "I know you showered at the hospital earlier, but would you like a bath now that you're home? I can send one of the girls up to draw you one."

"I don't need anyone to draw me a bath, and I don't want you to fuss over me. It's enough to know that you're here in case something goes wrong, so please go do whatever it is you need to do, and you can relax knowing I'll be here taking my first nap of the day."

Charlotte was relieved when Brando left the room. Her luggage had already been moved from her bedroom into his, and one of the maids brought up her briefcase and bags from the hospital. Once she was alone, she locked the bathroom door, stripped off her clothes and took a long soak in the deep tub. She washed her hair, rinsed and conditioned it, before climbing out and patting herself dry. With her long hair still wrapped in a towel, she climbed back into bed and fell asleep, grateful to be in a quiet room. Charlotte slept for over an hour and when she woke up, she discovered someone had placed a water bottle and glass next to the bed for her, plus a bowl of fresh fruit and a small plate of biscotti. But that wasn't all. Leaning against the lamp was a tall leather-bound book with a sticky note.

Charlotte, pick out your favorite.

She recognized the handwriting. Brando had written the note and she reached for the book and positioned it on her lap before opening the luxurious soft cream leather cover. *The Ricci-Baldi Bridal Collection*, the title page read.

Puzzled, Charlotte quickly flipped through the pages, from beginning to end. There were maybe twenty gowns in the book, and the entire book consisted of couture bridal gowns, exclusively designed by Livia, Brando's sister, and Livia's designer husband, Luca Baldi.

Brando wanted her to pick out her favorite bridal gown. Was this really happening?

She suddenly wasn't sure she could go through with the wedding, at least, not like this. She was scared, and troubled. Exhaling in a rush, she closed the design book, carefully replacing it where she'd found it, leaning against the glass lamp on the side table.

Intellectually she understood why marrying Brando was a good idea. But emotionally she couldn't see herself wearing a formal white gown, never mind a couture gown from one of Italy's top design teams. She wasn't having a dream wedding. The wedding was business, and the ceremony was for legal purposes. She and Brando were choosing to be responsible, and practical, and she didn't need a formal gown, or veil, or even flowers for that. She could wear a suit, or a smart dress, and Brando would wear one of his tailored suits, and they'd be married quietly, privately, by a government official without fuss.

It was better they not start their marriage under any illusions that this was a love marriage, because she had to manage her expectations, or beautiful, brilliant Brando Ricci would break her heart.

Brando returned from the winery to discover Charlotte had moved herself back to her bedroom.

He entered her bedroom with the briefest of knocks, annoyed that she'd go against his wishes. "What are you doing? Moving things around? Coming to rooms where you'll be alone at night?"

Charlotte drew the duvet up higher, hiding her breasts and bump. "I don't want or need constant supervision. I'm not a child. I'm having a child. Quite a significant distinction, Brando. And I didn't move anything but myself. Your staff carried my things, and I just took my time and walked back here."

He paced around the bed. "And what if something happens at night?"

"I'll call you. We both have phones. We're lucky to live in the age of technology."

He glared down at her. "I'm not amused. You're taking risks—"

"And you're being hopelessly overbearing," she interrupted, "as well as an alarmist. Dr. Leonardi said everything looked better, normal—"

"He never said 'normal.' He wanted you in the hospital. I was the one who insisted you would be able to rest better if you were at home. But I promised you'd be supervised."

"And I am. The midwife starts coming daily tomorrow. I'll have a quiet evening tonight. Just send a tray up for me and I'll have an early dinner, and will make an early night of it, too. I think having some downtime would be good for both of us."

Brando seemed about to protest when he thought better of it. He nodded shortly. "Fine." He started to leave, then turned in the doorway. "Did you see anything in Livia's designs that appealed to you? She's offered to come this weekend for a fitting."

The last thing Charlotte wanted to do was discuss the wedding, or a dress made for her by his famous sister, but she didn't want to offend him tonight. "There are so many beautiful designs, I couldn't even narrow the options down."

"No problem. I can look through them with you tomorrow."

"I don't need help looking at bridal gowns."

"Happy to give you my opinions."

"I'm sure you are. Good night, Brando."

"*Buona notte*, Charlotte."

CHAPTER EIGHT

A BREEZE RUSTLED the leaves of the citrus trees in the ornate terra-cotta pots on the terrace, and the moon, even though only a quarter full, winked white in the purple-black sky.

Brando leaned back in his chair at the table and let the beauty of the night distract him from Charlotte's lengthy explanation of why they didn't need a proper wedding, never mind a reception after.

She'd spent the last ten minutes giving detailed reasons why a formal wedding was a bad idea, and he let her talk as he sipped his after-dinner coffee. It was his favorite kind of night, warm, fragrant, without summer's sultry heat. He'd had a good day in the wineries, and Charlotte looked particularly beautiful tonight, too, wearing an ice-blue sleeveless blouse paired with crisp white silk trousers. Her long hair spilled over her shoulders, and she wore simple sapphire drop earrings that matched the blue of her eyes.

She was stunning and smart, and he felt fortunate that she was to be the mother of his children.

She'd be a good mother, a good partner and wife. If she'd just stop fighting him on the wedding. His family celebrated marriages, just as they celebrated births and anniversaries and other special moments.

"I want a proper ceremony, followed by a proper dinner, and a proper cake," he said. "This is our wedding. It should be special."

"Do we need the fuss, as well as the expense?"

"As this is the only wedding I will ever have, *yes*. It should be beautiful. Music, flowers, table decorations, all of it."

"A big wedding, Brando, really?"

"I didn't say 'big.' In fact, I want a small, intimate ceremony here at the *castello* chapel, followed by a reception in the courtyard. That way there is no traveling, no fuss, nothing to stress over, nor would you have to be on your feet very long."

Charlotte listened to his plans, and didn't know how to argue against them, especially as he offered to handle most of the arrangements so she didn't have to be stressed by anything. He did insist on her selecting a wedding dress, or at least, pointing out a few in the design book that she liked, and Livia and Luca would make up something special just for her.

"Your family knows, then?" she asked, careful to keep judgment from her voice.

"Only Livia so far. I will share the news with the rest once we have a wedding date."

Charlotte toyed with her dessert spoon. "What are you telling them?"

"That we're getting married and we'd love them to join us."

"Nothing about the pregnancy?"

"It's not the first thing I'll tell them, no." He lifted a brow, his expression slightly sardonic. "Would you prefer me to share the news about the baby first?"

"No." She glared at him. "And I don't want to wear a dress that screams 'pregnant bride,' either."

"I'm sure some of Livia's designs will flatter your figure. No matter what you'll wear, you'll look beautiful."

Charlotte's eyes suddenly smarted and she blinked, clearing her vision. "I feel rather lumpy at the moment, and I dread people talking. There will be gossip, you know. I know you don't care, but I'm not there yet. I'm still trying to figure out how to navigate this new world. My success stems from my reputation as someone who doesn't make mistakes. I fix other people's mistakes. And yet look at me—" She broke off, and bit into her lower lip, holding back the flow of words.

"Starting a family is a beautiful thing. We're excited. Remember that."

"You don't think your family will judge?"

"They'll be happy for us. They know you. They like you. Livia is thrilled to be making your dress."

"And your business associates? My clients?"

"They'll think the best, not the worst."

“Which is?”

“That we’re head over heels in love and eager to start our new lives together.” His silver gaze met hers and held. His voice dropped, and deepened. “And who is to say we’re not? Who is to say that this marriage isn’t something we both want?”

Her heart did a funny double beat, and butterflies filled her middle. She couldn’t look away from the flare of desire in his eyes, the heat radiating out, wrapping around her. “Marriage wasn't on the agenda,” she said.

“Maybe not, but you know I want you. If I could have you now, I would. Desire is not an issue between us.”

She could see heat and interest shimmering in his stunning pewter eyes. She felt the intense physical pull. She craved it herself, feeling isolated in this strange new body of hers, facing a different future than she’d ever imagined. “Then kiss me,” she whispered. “Make me remember why I lost my head over you.”

He drew her from her seat, up into his arms, one hand sliding beneath her hair to cup her nape as the other settled low on her hip. His lips covered hers, claiming her, his mouth warm, and firm. He smelled of that spice he wore and as well as a hint of wine. She welcomed the pressure of his mouth, her lips parting beneath his, his tongue tasting, teasing, sending shivers of pleasure through her. He kissed her until she felt boneless and mindless, kissing her until she forgot to breathe and she ached between her thighs, wanting pressure there. His knee moved between her legs, his hard thigh pressed to that place where she was so very sensitive. His hand ran up the length of her, over her hip and waist to cup her breast and then play with the tight, tender nipple, strumming the peaked tip so that she arched, grinding herself against him.

Pleasure screamed through her, bright, hot, intense.

She was so close to climaxing. Just another pinch of her nipple, another rub against his thigh, and she'd come. She wanted to come, craved release, but an orgasm could set off the contractions again.

Panting, Charlotte pulled back, feeling shameless and frustrated all at the same time. "I want you," she breathed, tears of vexation filling her eyes. "But I can't have you."

"You can, but not for a while."

"This is awful." She knocked away the tears, feeling wildly out of control. "We can marry but we can't have sex."

"We'll have sex again, I promise you. But you're right, we can't take any chances now. It's not worth the risk."

Charlotte couldn't fall asleep that night. She was spending so much time resting, so much time in bed, that she felt restless and trapped. The surging hormones didn't help. The relentless desire didn't help, either. She'd never felt sexual, but now, being so close to Brando, desire and awareness hummed through her night and day.

But what she felt for him was so much more than desire, and the feelings were growing stronger by the day. They hadn't even married and yet she felt bonded. Wed. Was it the pregnancy making her feel so connected to him, or was it the way he was treating her...as if she were special...priceless... irreplaceable?

And yes, right now, he was focused on her and the baby, but was it only because of the baby? How would things be after the baby was born?

Would Brando be as attentive? Would he still want her? Would he try to make her feel special?

She pictured Louisa—gorgeous, sexy, fun-loving Louisa—and felt a wave of insecurity. Charlotte hated feeling insecure. She'd had enough of that growing up in her family. It was impossible to get her parents' attention, impossible to get anyone's attention. She'd act out just to force one of the nannies to focus on her, hoping they'd take her to her parents, and yet when she was hauled before her parents, it never resulted in the outcome she'd wanted.

They had no time or patience for her when she was good, and they had even less time and patience when she was naughty. Gradually she learned not to look to others for affection, or validation. She would take care of herself, and learn to be happy and secure through her own actions and achievements. Once she stopped wanting her parents' love and approval, she discovered herself, and became the person she wanted to be.

Since arriving in Tuscany she felt lost, though, and wasn't sure who she was anymore.

She wasn't sure about marriage and forever, either. In her family marriage didn't equal forever. Marriage was just a source of friction and tension, with the friction growing worse until someone threw in the towel and initiated divorce.

The idea of marrying to divorce made her heartsick.

But being married to a man who didn't want her, and might have clandestine relationships on the side, would break her.

Charlotte couldn't escape her thoughts, or the panic rising in her, and she left bed and then left her room and headed upstairs to Brando's bedroom. It was well past midnight and she doubted he was awake but she needed to see him, needed to hear from him that they weren't making a terrible mistake.

She knocked lightly on his door and then opened it an inch. "Brando, are you sleeping?"

"Come in," he said, his voice deep and sleep roughened. "Are you unwell?"

"I'm fine," she said, stepping into his room, leaving the door slightly open behind her. "Everything's fine. I just can't sleep and my brain won't turn off and I'm getting myself worked up."

"Over what?"

"What if you don't like being married to me?" she whispered.

"Come here," he said, drawing back the covers, and patting the bed. "Crawl in with me."

She did, needing his warmth, craving security. He gave her a pillow and then pulled her close, her back to his chest, his arm wrapping around her middle, before bringing the light feather duvet over both of them.

"Do you want to talk?" he asked, his deep voice husky.

"Will you regret marrying me?"

"We're making a family. I will never regret having a family."

A lump filled her throat. It wasn't quite the reassurance she needed. "What about me, though? Will you regret marrying me?"

He kissed her bare shoulder. "Never."

Her chest squeezed, air bottling in her lungs. "Promise?"

"It will not always be easy between us. We're two strong people. But we can make it work, if we want to make it work. Does that make sense?"

"Yes."

He pushed her hair aside and kissed the back of her neck. "We will find our happiness, *cara*. I am sure of that."

And wrapped in his arms, and in his assurances, Charlotte fell asleep.

The wedding plans moved forward quickly, with the date set for the last Saturday in June, which was less than two weeks away.

Brando handled the arrangements, but he ran his ideas past her, making sure she approved. She liked his ideas and agreed with him on virtually everything, appreciating his logic, his tastes, as well as his decisiveness. Her only real objection was marrying in the historic chapel. Charlotte asked if maybe they couldn't say their vows outside, perhaps in one of the gardens, with a view of the valley.

He agreed with her suggestion for a simple outdoor ceremony, and shared his idea for a reception in the inner courtyard, which could be illuminated with strings of white lights, and torches attached to the stone walls.

Ten days before the wedding, Livia arrived to take measurements for Charlotte's dress, but before they could discuss dresses, there were other things Livia wanted to know. "You and Brando did not seem to like each other very much during our meetings. Clearly the rest of us did not know what was really going on behind closed doors."

Charlotte blushed. "Nothing happened during our work together. He and I did have some issues—"

"Too much chemistry, hmm?"

"There were sparks, yes," Charlotte admitted. "But nothing happened while I was under contract. I wouldn't do that to you, not while working for you. It happened New Year's Eve. He'd invited me to Enzo's big party. That was the first time—and the only time—we got together."

"One night and you're pregnant?"

Charlotte grimaced. "We used protection, too. He did, I did." She gestured helplessly to the bump. "But this one wanted to be born."

"That's a Ricci for you," Livia answered with a wink. "Prepare yourself. You're going to have your hands full. Now let's get your measurements and discuss the kind of dress you'd like for the wedding."

"I don't actually have a preference," Charlotte admitted. "I prefer clean, sophisticated designs, which is what you do. Can I just leave it to you to make whatever you think would look best on me?"

Livia embraced her, and then kissed her on each cheek. "It would be my pleasure. Leave it to me."

A week passed, and the wedding was just days away. The guest list had swelled, with most of Brando's family electing to stay overnight at the *castello* rather than make the drive back to Florence. All the decisions had been made for the wedding, too. Musicians and photographer were booked, flowers ordered, and Brando's chef from Florence was coming to assist the *castello* chef and kitchen staff for the wedding weekend.

All the decisions that needed to be made were done. But Brando, who wasn't a worrier, had concerns. The wedding, while still intimate, was no longer as small as he'd hoped, and the family and friends coming would be up late into the night, celebrating. Brando had wanted a special night for Charlotte, a wedding they'd both remember for years to come. He just hoped that it wasn't going to be too much for her. The last thing they needed was Charlotte being rushed back to the hospital at the end of their wedding night.

From her room Charlotte could see the preparations for the ceremony and reception this weekend. The villa staff swept and scrubbed the courtyard, wiping down stones and the dozen columns supporting the arches of the inner courtyard. Planters were refreshed, topiaries pruned, and long strings of white lights were run across the courtyard, creating a tent-like canopy.

The morning of the wedding, tables were set up in the interior courtyard, and then covered with white cloths. Flowers arrived, and antique silver candelabra lined the long tables, the heavy silver candleholders matching the ornate silverware.

Livia was there to help her dress, and after her hair and makeup were done by a stylist Livia had brought from Florence, Charlotte carefully stepped into her gown.

Her gown was exquisite and what made it so beautiful was that it was perfect for her. It was her style—modern, clean and yet classic. The white silk gleamed in the sunlight, and the luxurious fabric molded to her full breasts, hugging her torso and bump, before forming a full, sophisticated skirt. There were even pockets in the skirt, a touch she adored. Normally she would have avoided such a deep plunging neckline, and yet the dramatic neckline, paired with the wide shoulder straps, looked chic, and drew the eye from her bump to her shoulders and face.

With her hair pinned up, and a long white veil attached to the chignon, she looked like a true bride—radiant, glowing, excited.

Livia walked around Charlotte, adjusting her skirt, and then the floor-length veil. "Perfection," she said approvingly. "Even the pearl earrings. Elegant, classic, discrete."

Charlotte reached up and touched one pearl stud. "My mother's."

"Is she coming?"

Charlotte shook her head. "She couldn't make it. Most of my family couldn't make it. One of my sisters is on the way. She's coming from London with her husband. They're not here yet, but I think they should arrive soon."

"Not to worry. You have lots of family here," Livia answered. "The Riccis are here. You are one of us now."

In the end, Charlotte thought her wedding was impossibly beautiful, although it wasn't as small as Brando had intimated. Her sister and brother-in-law arrived moments before she walked down the aisle, and of course, all of Brando's family was there—his mother, his mother's sister, his brothers and sister, cousins, so many cousins, plus other guests, people who were "like family" to the Riccis.

They said their vows in the garden overlooking the valley with the gently rolling hills, dark green vineyards and views of the tiled roofs of the village below, and then moved to the *castello*'s courtyard for the dinner and music. The flowers on the table matched her bridal bouquet—the palest pink roses hand-tied with a wide pale pink satin ribbon.

She felt beautiful in the dress Livia had made for her, and Brando looked impossibly handsome in his black suit with the white shirt and dark tie. His hair was sleekly combed back, highlighting his strong cheekbones, jaw and lovely mouth. Her hand had trembled in his as they'd said the vows, but his voice was deep and steady, and he'd held her gaze the entire time, promising to honor and protect her for the rest of their lives.

During dinner Brando insisted she stay seated at the head table, asking guests to come to her. She wondered what he'd said to them as no one seemed surprised, or questioned why she left her chair only to cut the cake, and have a first dance with Brando. The song from the first dance was the same song they'd danced to on New Year's Eve, "At Last" by Etta James. Charlotte was surprised he'd remembered, but also touched. Dancing with him beneath the stars and moon and strings of white lights was probably one of the most romantic moments in her life. Brando might not love her, but he'd gone to great pains to make tonight special. To make her feel special.

"You take my breath away," he said, as the song came to an end.

"Thank you for a beautiful wedding, and a beautiful night," she answered.

His head dropped and he kissed her, there in front of everyone. The kiss filled her with warmth and hope. Their families and friends applauded. Brando lifted his head and grinned. She blushed and smiled.

And then before she knew it was all over, Brando was saying he needed to carry his bride away, and he encouraged everyone to eat and drink and dance as late as they wanted as there were no neighbors nearby to disturb.

Brando literally carried her away, too, sweeping her into his arms and carrying her through the courtyard doors and up the central staircase to his room on the third floor.

She'd been here before but she'd never seen it like this. Tonight, the master bedroom glowed with dozens of white candles. They were everywhere—on the mantel, on tables, on windowsills. There were roses, too, countless white roses, and across the bed lay a delicate ivory satin nightgown with an ivory satin-and-lace robe.

"A gift from Livia," Brando said, putting her down next to the bed. "She said every bride needs something special to wear for her wedding night."

Charlotte suddenly felt overwhelmed by the

beauty of the day, and the kindness of Brando's sister, as well as everyone's goodwill. Their guests had been happy for them, celebrating their marriage with toasts, hugs and laughter. "Livia has completely spoiled me," she said, reaching to lightly stroke the satin nightgown. "I hope she knows I'm so very grateful."

"She does." He watched her from the foot of the bed. "How do you feel?"

"Good. A little tired. But happy." She looked at him, and smiled, tears in her eyes. "Thank you for tonight. It was beautiful, all of it, and I'm—"

"Grateful," he interrupted, finishing her words for her. "Yes, I know." His mouth quirked. "But I didn't do this for your gratitude. This was for us, and our son, so we'd have memories and photos to share with our children and grandchildren, and then they can say, *Oh, you were so young!*"

She smiled. "Well, thank you for giving us memories." She glanced down at the shimmering satin nightgown. "I guess I should change."

"Let me help you out of your gown, and then I need to get something from the library and I'll be back."

She turned around and he made quick work of the dozens of small hooks hidden in the seam of her gown. The bodice fell away and she caught the silk, pressing it against her breasts to keep from exposing herself.

"I have seen you naked before," he said, a hint of amusement in his deep voice.

She blushed. “Not like this. There is so much more of me now.”

“I think you’re absolutely beautiful pregnant.”

She didn’t know what to say, and so she stood up on tiptoe, and kissed him. He caught her by the arms and pulled her closer, his mouth claiming hers, hunger and heat and possession in the kiss. Desire shot through her, bright and fierce. She wanted him badly, wanted the pressure and sensation, wanted touch and release. Everything in her craved more of him—more of his time, more of his attention, more of his heart.

She loved him, and yet she feared the love because she didn’t know how she’d ever survive this marriage if he didn’t love her back.

Brando lifted his head, gazed down into her eyes, before pressing the pad of his thumb to her full, tender lips. “There are so many things I want to do to you. It’s incredibly difficult to keep my hands off you.”

It wasn’t a declaration of love, but it was something, she thought, as he left the room and she removed her veil, and unpinned her hair, brushing it smooth before taking a bath and changing into her satin nightgown, the delicate fabric impossibly soft and light as it followed her every curve.

Brando returned, and his dinner jacket was off, and the tie gone. He’d unbuttoned his dress shirt, exposing the upper planes of his muscular, golden chest. He was carrying a bottle and two crystal flutes. “Come,” he said, going to the French doors and opening them onto his private balcony.

She followed him out, smiling as he popped the cork from the champagne and filled the two flutes. “Just a sip,” he admonished, handing her one flute. “Just for a toast.”

She took the pretty flute and glanced down at the pale gold champagne, the bubbles rising and popping.

“To you,” he said, lifting his glass. “To your beauty, to your amazing mind, to the miracle you carry. I’m lucky to call you my partner, and wife.”

Her eyes burned and a lump filled her throat. “Thank you,” she whispered, lightly touching her glass to his.

As she sipped her champagne, a loud popping sound came from the corner of the castle, and then fireworks filled the sky, a dazzling display of light.

She could hear their guests cheering below, and Brando reached for her, and kissed her as the dark sky lit up with all the colors of the rainbow. It was an extraordinary surprise, and a wonderful way to cap a magical evening.

He’d given her absolutely everything this evening but his heart.

CHAPTER NINE

THE *CASTELLO* WAS still full of guests the next day, with Brando's friends and family staying over to enjoy a leisurely Sunday morning brunch before an afternoon departure.

Charlotte came downstairs for the late breakfast, hoping to see her sister Alice, but Alice and Philip had already left to catch their flight back to London. Charlotte felt a pinch of disappointment, aware that she'd exchanged only a dozen words with her sister last night, but at least Alice and Philip had appeared to be having fun, sitting at the same table with Brando's brothers, and talking the evening away with Marcello and Elena, Marcello's wife.

Elena and Livia were together, drinking coffee, and Elena waved Charlotte over now. "Last night was beautiful," Elena said to Charlotte as she joined them at their table. "And those fireworks! Did you know?"

"No, it was a complete surprise," Charlotte answered. "I was shocked, but I shouldn't have been.

Brando did most of the planning for the wedding and it went off perfectly."

"It did," Livia agreed. "And you were the most radiant bride. Brando couldn't keep his eyes from you."

Charlotte grimaced. "He watches me constantly, afraid that I might go into labor." She saw her sister-in-laws' confused expressions and explained, "We had a scare a couple weeks ago. If Brando hadn't flown me back to Florence in his helicopter, who knows what would have happened. But fortunately we got there quickly and the doctors could stop the labor. That's why he's so protective of me now. We want the baby to stay put as long as possible."

Elena glanced at Livia, murmuring, "Aren't you glad Brando married her, and not the other one? That would have been awful."

Livia gave her head a slight shake, discouraging Elena, before smiling warmly at Charlotte. "We've been hoping he'd settle down, and so very glad it's you. We're already quite fond of you."

"And we also know you're not after his money like the other one," Elena added. "Thank goodness Marcello convinced Brando to take a paternity test before the wedding—"

"The wedding?" Charlotte interrupted. "Was Brando engaged before?"

Elena looked at Livia. "Would you call it an engagement, Liv? I don't think it was that formal. She was pregnant and he was going to marry her. Wasn't that pretty much how it was?"

Charlotte's heart fell, and her insides went icy cold. She clasped her hands together, feeling chilled to the bone. "When was this?"

"A couple of years ago," Elena answered. "I don't even know what's happened to her—"

"I thought the flowers were gorgeous last night," Livia said, cutting Elena off. "They were roses and peonies, weren't they?"

Charlotte nodded vaguely, unable to focus on the question. Brando had been through all of this before? He'd nearly married another woman because he thought she was pregnant, and apparently, all his family had known.

And here he was, years later, going through it all again. No wonder he was good at planning weddings. The whole celebration last night had been a show…a sham…

My God, what had his whole family been thinking last night as they watched him marry her? Charlotte put a hand to her middle, suddenly feeling as though she might be sick. "I think I need to get some food," she said unsteadily, rising. "If you'll excuse me, I'll see what I can find."

She waited until late afternoon and everyone had gone before approaching Brando about what she'd learned from Elena and Livia. She found him in his ground-floor study so lined with antique volumes that it probably was a former library. He was at his desk, reading through a document, looking relaxed and bronzed as if he'd spent his afternoon swimming.

He looked up with a smile as she entered the room with its golden paneling and rich wood accents. "How was your rest?"

"Boring." She took a seat across from his desk. "Not very restful." She hesitated, trying to figure out how to broach the subject that had troubled her all day. The more she'd thought about it, the more upset she became. "I heard a story today," she said carefully. "Elena told me. But Livia was there and verified it. Apparently they nearly got a different sister-in-law a couple of years ago. Elena says they didn't like her much. Thankfully she likes me more." Charlotte stared at a button on Brando's shirt, unable to meet his eyes. "It was a bit embarrassing to realize you've been through all this before—"

"I haven't."

"Apparently, you have. You get a woman pregnant, and you marry her."

"I've never been married before. There have been no weddings, no engagements, no babies. You're the first."

"But this other woman… You would have married her if it had been your baby?"

"Yes."

Her heart did that awful freefall again, plummeting all the way to her feet. Charlotte wasn't special. He had no real feelings for her. Brando was just going through the motions.

"But Charlotte, it wasn't mine. We didn't marry.

None of this is relevant," he said, leaning forward in his seat. "You can't let Elena upset you over something so trivial—"

"Trivial?" Charlotte interrupted. "Marriage changes everything, and marrying you has turned my life inside out. Having a baby would have been a significant change, but this...becoming your wife... moving to Tuscany... I've given up everything I am, and everything I've known, for you—"

"Not for me, for our child, for our family."

"No, Brando," she corrected, getting to her feet, hands clasped tightly together. "I agreed to marriage because I would be marrying you. Just for clarification, I wouldn't have married anyone else. I married you because it's you."

She left his study then, and headed outside to walk the rose garden, and then circle the *castello* grounds, ending up near the fountain in the historic walled garden.

Brando found her in the walled garden, pacing around the gravel like a caged animal. "The walking doesn't seem to be calming you."

She shot him a look of reproach. "I'm not calm, no."

"You're getting yourself agitated over nothing. Charlotte, there was no one else—"

"Oh, Brando, please. Don't say that. Let's not pretend there has never been anyone before me. Your bed is never empty. You never lack for female company."

"When I'm in a serious, monogamous relationship, it's serious and monogamous."

"Define 'serious relationship,'" she said, hands on her hips as she faced him.

"Affection, attachment, respect, monogamous."

"Is that what we have?"

"You're my wife. My family."

His words were beginning to make her feel a little mad. "Yes, but you feel affection, attachment, respect for me?"

"Yes."

"We're to be faithful to each other?"

"Yes, absolutely."

"And this is what you offer your significant others? This is the most you offer? Affection, attachment, respect?"

His jaw set, his eyes narrowed. "Last night you were content with me, and hopeful about the future. Today, you throw it all back in my face? Because Elena thoughtlessly mentioned someone from my past?"

Furious tears burned the back of her eyes. "I'm not a replacement bride—"

"No, you're not. But I don't know what you want from me, Charlotte. I don't even know how to talk to you right now. We had a beautiful wedding last night. We had our friends and family here. You thanked me last night for making it a special day, but suddenly, based on something Elena said, it's not enough?"

She didn't know how to explain, but she felt as if

there was an injustice here. In marrying him, she'd lost everything she'd known—her home, her name, her identity, her independence. And he'd lost nothing other than his ability to sleep with whomever he wanted. Because he hadn't really given up anything. He didn't have to change, or even feel too much, because he didn't feel too much.

"This was a mistake," she said hoarsely, mouth dry, stomach in knots. "I didn't marry out of duty. It's not why I agreed to this."

"We're doing this for our son," he answered.

"This marriage will make us miserable. I refuse to raise a baby in a home where we're miserable."

"I'm not miserable."

"Because you don't love. You lust—"

"Charlotte."

"Where are your emotions? And what do you really feel for me? Affection…desire?"

"Yes."

"It's not enough."

"Our attachment will grow."

She was already attached, though. She already cared. What was she supposed to do, wait for him to catch up? Hope he might one day have more feelings for her?

"I don't want this marriage," she said lowly. "I don't want to be part of any of this. You're not who I thought you were. We don't have what I thought we have."

He closed the distance between them, hands settling on her upper arms. "You're working yourself up over nothing. Adele meant nothing to me. I swear—"

"Isn't that the whole issue?" she cried, looking up into his face. "You don't care about any of them you've been with. You love sex, the act of sex, but you don't love the women you're with, and you will never love me." She tried to pull away but he didn't release her. Charlotte pushed his chest, and still he held her. "See, it's already a trap. I'm trapped. I knew this would happen. It's what marriage does… It changes people… changes the power balance between two people."

He gave her a gentle shake. "Nothing has changed, Charlotte."

Her chest burned and her heart was beating so fast she couldn't catch her breath. Her emotions were chaotic, her control splintering. Where was the Charlotte who was so capable of dealing with crises that she could virtually do it in her sleep? She needed that Charlotte to show up, right now. "I shouldn't have agreed to marry you. I shouldn't have let you convince me it was the right thing to do. It's not, and I can't pretend like you, can't fake happiness." She struggled to pluck his fingers from her arm. "I can't live with you. I won't live with you—"

"The baby—"

"The baby will be fine. I promise you I'll make sure of that." She reached up and pressed a hand to her eyes to hold back the tears. She wouldn't cry now. She had to keep it together. "I'd like to return to Florence. I'll get a small apartment for the rest of the summer—"

"That's absurd."

"I'll be close to the hospital should anything happen," she added, continuing as if he hadn't interrupted. "I promise to keep you informed. I won't take any risks. You won't have to worry about me."

"I don't understand any of this."

"That's the problem, Brando. You don't understand this, because you don't understand me. I didn't marry you to give the baby your name. I didn't marry you to do the right thing. I married you because—" She broke off, tears filling her eyes. "I married you because I wanted to be with you."

"And that's changed?"

She couldn't hold the tears back. *"Yes."*

"Why? Because you've heard some story about Adele and her pregnancy that had nothing to do with me?"

"You were prepared to marry her. You would have married her—"

"It wasn't my child. I didn't get her pregnant."

"It doesn't matter. What matters is that we're all interchangeable in your eyes. You love making love, but you don't really love, and then when you're faced with the consequences, you think you're doing the right thing, but marriage isn't the answer, not when there's no love."

"It's a little late for regrets, though. We've said our vows, we've made a commitment. There's no backing out of it now." He released her then and she took a step back, and then another, her chin high, spine straight.

For a long moment she just held his gaze, expression defiant, before regally turning around and walking away from him, aware that his gaze followed her every step of the way.

Brando watched Charlotte return to the *castello*, gut on fire, head throbbing. What the hell had just happened?

How had everything gone sideways?

She'd been happy last night, radiant in her bridal gown, and breathtaking in her shimmering satin nightgown. He'd slept with one arm around her last night, savoring her warmth, her softness, feeling overwhelmed with his desire to protect her. And then the baby kicked, right against his hand where it rested on her belly, and he'd known then that he would sacrifice everything for them, his wife and son. They would want for nothing. They would always have him, a devoted husband and father.

All day he'd felt renewed. Purposeful. There was a reason now for him to work harder, to push to be more successful. Everything he did would be for them… And yet Charlotte now wanted none of it.

And nothing from him.

He was baffled, but also angry. Angry that she

didn't trust him. Angry that she would judge and condemn him. Angry that she'd be so selfish that she'd put her needs before their son's needs...before the needs of the family.

Apparently, he didn't know her.

Apparently, she wasn't who he'd thought she was, either.

There was no honeymoon, and they spent the next week living like strangers in the *castello*. Charlotte moved out of the master bedroom and back into hers. He never once commented on her decision.

After she returned to her own room, they still had dinner together twice, but each evening they barely spoke, the atmosphere tense, so severely strained that Charlotte couldn't manage a bite. After the second miserable dinner, she told him she couldn't eat with him anymore, it was too upsetting, and it was true. After that last dinner, she threw up after crying so hard. This wasn't the life she wanted. This wasn't the marriage she'd agreed to.

Days passed and the first week of July had come and gone, the summer heat making the air hot, and heavy. The heat gave Charlotte a headache and she stayed in her room, in the dark, heavy coral silk curtains drawn to keep her room cool and dim.

She felt listless and lost, confused as to why she was here in this place, living this way. Brando didn't seem to care that he never saw her anymore, either, and he came to her room only after hearing she hadn't gotten out of bed again one day.

He didn't bother knocking. He opened her bedroom door, stood on the threshold, gaze sweeping the room, before crossing the floor and drawing back the heavy silk drapes, allowing sunlight to pierce the darkness. "Are you having contractions? Is there pain?" he asked brusquely.

"No," she whispered.

"Then what are you doing still in bed?"

"I'm on bed rest, Brando."

"The midwife said you should get up and walk a little. She said you need fresh air."

"I'm fine."

"You're not fine." He crossed to the side of the bed, narrowed gaze raking her, the curl of his upper lip revealing disdain.

"I want you to get up."

"Why?" she asked, rolling onto her back to look up at him.

"Because this isn't good for you, or the baby."

She hated his tone, hated his arrogance, hated his superiority. She pushed herself up, the covers heavy on her legs. "Do you only care about the baby?"

He rolled his eyes. "That's absurd, and you know it. I care about you. I'm concerned about you. You can't keep this up. It's not healthy, and it's not good for any of us—"

"You don't seem overly troubled by it. You've

gone about your life this past week without any trouble."

"I was giving you space."

"Thank you for the profound emptiness."

"I was respecting your wishes."

"You don't know me at all, do you?"

"I don't play games. I didn't think you played them, either."

"You're above all of this, aren't you? How nice not to have emotions—"

"Charlotte, I'm genuinely worried about you. You're clearly having a breakdown of some sort."

She stared at him in wonderment. "What is your solution to the problem, then, Brando?"

"Get some sun, go for a swim, take short walks, read something interesting, take the focus off you." His broad shoulders shifted carelessly. "You're not the only one whose life has changed. We both have adjustments to make."

"And yet this is your house, and your country. You are surrounded by your family and your employees, and your friends. The only thing you have lost is your ability to bed new women." Her lips curved, but it wasn't a smile. The pain inside her was blistering and raw. "Is that your hardship, Brando?"

Brando couldn't remember the last time he was this angry. He felt as if he'd married a stranger. Who was this woman in his house? What had happened to the Charlotte he knew? Where was the woman he'd been so enamored with? "Do I need to call the doctor?" he asked, struggling to contain his temper. "Should I make an appointment for tomorrow?"

She averted her face. Her lower lip quivered. "I'm not sick."

"Something is clearly wrong, though. You're not yourself. If you don't try to pull yourself together, then I'll find help."

"You don't need to find 'help,'" she said, still not looking at him. "I'll be fine once I'm away from here. I need a break. I need to go somewhere for a while. I'm suffocating here."

"No, I'm not going to let you go 'somewhere.' You're not running away. You've made a commitment. We both made a commitment, and we're going to honor the commitment."

Her head jerked around. Her gaze met his, eyes flashing fire. "You're not my father. I don't work for you. I don't belong to you, which means you don't get to tell me what to do, or how to behave."

"You're my wife. That gives me some authority—"

"Authority?" she laughed. "Oh, that's fascinating, but also wrong. You have no authority over me, and you trying to manage me will backfire. It'll destroy everything I feel for you."

"Obviously, you feel very little if you're already determined to leave me."

"Speaking of feeling very little, Brando, just because you throw huge sums of money around doesn't mean you're being kind or loving. It means you're paying for things, but I don't need your money, and I don't need you to buy things for me, and you can't buy me. Maybe everyone else is taken in by your extravagance and generosity but I know the truth. You dazzle with your gifts and your generosity, because it's all you offer. Our elegant wedding…the dinner reception…even the fireworks… It was to make up for the fact that you don't love me, and you will never love me. Instead I'm supposed to be satisfied—"

"You don't know what you're saying." His hands balled into fists. He was at the end of his tether.

"No? Then tell me about one woman from your past that you deeply loved. Tell me how it broke your heart when it ended, and you didn't think you'd ever be able to continue without her."

"This is ridiculous. You're hysterical. It's not good for you, and it's not good for the baby. Clearly you need space, space I'm happy to give to you. I'll be heading out to the vineyard near Greve and then having dinner with my winemakers. I'll have my phone with me. Call if there's an emergency. Otherwise I'll check in on you after I'm back."

Hands bunched in the covers, heart thudding hard, Charlotte watched him leave her room, and listened to him close her door, firmly.

Part of her wanted to fling pillows at the door. Part of her wanted to hurl insults at him, because who was he to tell her anything? Who was he to lecture her on behavior? He was the one who'd slept with legions of women, never truly caring for any of them. But on the other hand, she'd known who he was when they went to bed together. She knew he was a powerful, sexual man who had no intentions of settling down.

If she wanted to cast blame, she could only blame herself for falling for him, and worse, allowing herself to become so terribly attached. The attachment, the love, the passion… It was what made her hurt now. It was maddening that she felt so much for him, and he felt nothing at all.

The dinner with his winemakers went later than he anticipated and the *castello* was dark when he returned. Brando locked the front door and headed upstairs, hesitating on the second landing, wondering if he should still check on Charlotte at this late hour.

There was no light shining beneath her door and he remembered their fight earlier. Perhaps it was better to let her sleep. She needed sleep, and so did he. He'd have breakfast with her in the morning and begin working on untangling their knotted relationship, because ignoring her, and their problems, hadn't worked so far.

The next morning Brando asked his housekeeper if Charlotte had requested a breakfast tray yet. The housekeeper looked at him, expression bewildered.

"She left yesterday, signor," she said. "A car came for her a little after you left."

Brando didn't believe it. He went through his room, and then her former bedroom, but all traces of her were gone. He called her but her phone was turned off, and he was sent to voice mail. Brando struggled to stay calm as he threw his things into his leather duffel to return to Florence.

He spent the drive to Florence trying her phone—still off—before making some calls. She wasn't at his house in Florence. She hadn't checked back in at the hotel she'd stayed at before. Florence was a city filled with hotels. She could be anywhere.

He called a half-dozen hotels while he drove, and none of them had her under her name, or even his.

His frustration mounted with every call. This was ridiculous. Such a waste of time, as well as dangerous for her and their son. She was supposed to be on modified bed rest, not running off somewhere making it difficult for her to be found.

In Florence, he went straight to his house, asked his staff to help make discreet calls, but even after two days no one could find a trace of her. Brando was certain she wouldn't try to fly, not in her condition, but where had she gone? And why? Why go through the motions of marrying him, if she'd never intended to stay?

Those questions haunted him over the next week and continued to trouble him for the rest of the summer as it seemed Charlotte had vanished completely.

CHAPTER TEN

TWO MONTHS WENT by, two months without a word from Charlotte, months that passed with agonizing slowness for Brando.

Where had she gone?

And why had she cut him out so completely?

He knew she'd seen Dr. Leonardi at least three times over the past eight weeks, because ten days ago Brando had cornered the doctor and demanded information. Dr. Leonardi didn't know where Charlotte was staying, but he confirmed that she'd come in for her regular appointments and all was well.

So Charlotte was in the area still—that was a plus.

But where, he didn't know, and he couldn't find her, despite repeated searches. Knowing she'd remained in Florence helped calm him, though. He still didn't understand why she'd leave, but he was grateful she wasn't taking unnecessary risks by traveling.

The baby's due date was September 24. If it wasn't harvest season, he'd be permanently in the

Florence town house, but as harvesting had begun, he was at the *castello* in Chianti, waiting for word, should word come that she'd gone into labor.

Word arrived far earlier than he expected, though. It was just the first week of September when Brando received a call from Livia telling him to get to the hospital immediately, that Charlotte had gone into labor.

It was on the tip of his tongue to ask how Livia found out, but instead he hung up and drove straight to the hospital. Thankfully it was the middle of the day and there was no traffic, and he made it to the Florence hospital in under an hour.

Brando was met in the emergency waiting room by Livia. "There are complications," Livia said bluntly. "They've taken her to surgery."

"The baby?"

"Is fine. He's here, small, but healthy. It's Charlotte. She's hemorrhaging. They're trying to save her now."

Brando shook his head. "What do you mean, *save her*?"

"Her blood pressure dropped very quickly. Her heart—"

"You're not making sense."

"Because you're not listening. Charlotte is in critical condition, and I was told to prepare you—"

"Prepare me for what?"

"She might not make it, Brando. The surgeons

are going to do the best they can, but there was a lack of blood flow to her vital organs."

"I need to see her."

"You can't. She's in surgery."

"I'm her husband, Livia."

Livia gave him a pitying look. "And what will you do once you're there? How can you do anything to help her?"

"You don't think I should be with her?"

"Where have you been all summer?"

He froze, and then slowly turned to stare at his sister. "What do you know about this?"

"I've taken care of her all summer." Livia lifted her chin. "She's been with me."

"I've been to your house. She wasn't there."

"She's been staying in the apartment over my studio. I've been taking her meals and making sure she gets to her doctor appointments. My daughter has been helping, too, keeping her company so she wouldn't be lonely when I had to work."

"You never told me."

"Charlotte asked me not to."

"Why?"

"She was terribly unhappy. She needed a friend."

"I am her husband."

"Yes, but not her friend."

Livia's reproach stung. His hands knotted. "You shouldn't have gone behind my back."

"What would you rather I did? Turn my back on my new sister, pregnant with your baby? Tell her

I don't care? But I care, and I took her in, because I know somewhere in your hard heart, you care."

"I do not have a hard heart, and I have always cared. I was never unkind, never impatient—"

"But was there love?"

"Of course there was love. She's my wife, the mother of my son."

Livia sighed. "Brando, you're so very shrewd in so many areas, but you don't understand women, and you don't understand Charlotte. Charlotte loves you, so much so that I think she's dying because her heart is breaking."

"She's not dying."

Livia's shoulders twisted. "Fine. You know best. You know everything."

Her icy, dismissive tone gave him pause. "You're not being dramatic?"

She shot him a look of scorn. "You have a newborn son, and a wife dying. Why should I be dramatic?"

"I don't know," he admitted. "Maybe I'm in shock."

"Then prepare yourself. It's probably going to get worse."

His chest tightened, his pulse felt heavy and slow. "She can't die. We have a son—"

"You'll find another wife. It'll be fine."

Brando drew back, appalled, sickened. "What in God's name?"

"Her heart stopped, Brando. It will be a miracle if she makes it. But you'll find someone else to marry and raise Charlotte's son—"

Brando walked away from her then, going to the nurses' desk and demanding to be allowed into the surgical room. "I'll scrub in. I need to be there. My wife needs me."

"That's not permitted, signor. I'm sorry—"

He dropped his voice, speaking in measured words. "I am one of the largest benefactors for this hospital. I'm not asking to participate in surgery, but to be allowed to be in the room. I will not interfere with anyone. I just need to be near her."

The nurse said she'd check, but she couldn't promise anything.

Brando refused to look at his sister while he waited for the nurse to return. Brando watched the hands on the clock slowly move. It seemed to take forever for the nurse to return, but it was maybe just five minutes.

"They're just finishing now. She's to be taken to ICU, where they will monitor her recovery. I'll take you to her once she's there. It will be another ten, maybe fifteen minutes."

"So, she's okay? She's stable?"

"I wasn't given any information about her condition, only that she's to be closely monitored." The nurse hesitated. "Would you like to see your son, though? I can take you to him until you're able to join your wife."

Brando stood at the window of the neonatal intensive care unit staring at his son in the Isolette. His son looked tiny and red-faced, swaddled in a blue-and-white blanket with a little blue knit cap on his head.

A nurse joined him outside the window to explain that the incubator was protecting the baby from infections, allergens and excessive noise. He'd had a stressful delivery and the hospital was doing what it could to regulate his environment with optimum oxygen, humidity and warmth. "It's a lot to go from his mother into the outside world," the nurse said with a smile. "But overall he's doing well." She shot him a side-glance. "It's his mother we're worrying about. How is she?"

"I don't know yet. I'm supposed to go to her once she's in recovery."

"Let me make a call."

The wait again felt endless, and Brando stared at his son, unable to imagine his child growing up without his mother. Without Charlotte.

He couldn't imagine life without Charlotte. She was meant to be with him, part of everything. She was part of him. How could she go? How could there be a future without her?

Brando's gut burned, and the fire spread to his chest, creating a searing pain. None of this made sense.

How had they even gotten to this point?

And yet how had he thought this would turn out?

The nurse returned. "I'll take you to her."

Charlotte might have been taken to recovery from surgery, but she wasn't awake. She lay utterly still, her skin so pale that it looked like alabaster. Tubes were attached, as well as machines that monitored her.

Her long hair had been gathered into a side ponytail, the vivid gold strands the only color against the white sheets.

The nurse who'd walked him to ICU stood next to him for a moment. "She'll remain sedated for some time," she said quietly. "Don't expect anything."

Brando gave a brief nod that he'd heard the nurse, but he couldn't look away from his wife. He still couldn't process it all. That she'd been with Livia all this time. That his family had been taking her meals and keeping her company. That even his mother had been to see her.

Everyone had been with her but him.

The nurse silently slipped out and Brando drew a chair close to the bed. He watched the shallow rise and fall of her chest, watched the pulse at the base of her throat, watched the monitors measuring her every breath and beat of her heart.

She looked so small and fragile. So terribly alone.

Regret filled him, regret and pain. He'd caused her pain, and everyone could see it, and everyone could feel it, and everyone wanted to do something about it...everyone, it seemed, but him.

Brando slipped his hand through the tubes and

cords and covered her hand with his, careful not to bump or disturb anything attached to her.

Carefully, gently he squeezed her hand. Of course, there was no response, and yet her very lack of response drove home how vulnerable she was. How vulnerable they all were.

"We made a beautiful baby," he said to her, voice low and rough. "He's in the nursery where they're taking good care of him. But he needs you, *cara*. You are his everything. You're the only one he knows. You're the only one he loves. He trusts you. He depends on you. Don't leave him, Charlotte. Don't break his heart."

There was no response from her, no flicker of her eyelids, no movement in her fingers. She was so still it was as if she was no longer there.

And yet she was here. She was somewhere in there, resting, quiet, waiting.

Waiting for what?

He thought of Livia's words. *But was there love?*

He'd answered that of course there was love. He married her. He was starting a family with her.

Charlotte loves you, so much I think she's dying because her heart is breaking...

But that didn't make sense. He loved Charlotte. It's why he'd followed her to Los Angeles. It's why he wanted her in his life—forever. How could she not know how he felt? How could she not believe he cared deeply?

He stood up, and leaned over her, gently kissing

her forehead. "It's not just the baby that needs you, *cara.* I need you," he whispered, his lips brushing her cheek, and then her lips. "I love you. I always have. I always will. Now come back to me. You've made your point. I'm paying attention. Give me a chance to make it right."

She woke late that night, groggy and weak, but her eyes opened, and she saw him and for a long moment just stared at him. "The baby?" she croaked, voice raspy. "How is he?"

Brando left the chair he'd been in all day, all night, and stood next to her. "Good. But he'll probably be happier once he's with you."

"He's really all right?"

"Yes." He could see the fear in her eyes as well as the extreme fatigue. She'd been given transfusions, but she was still pale, dark shadows etched beneath her eyes. "You're the one we're worrying about."

"I'm fine."

And yet her voice sounded hollow and there was no light in her eyes. She wasn't fine. She hurt. She didn't feel safe, didn't feel loved. He felt an ache in his chest, hating that all this time he'd caused her so much pain. "I have missed you," he said. "I looked for you everywhere. I called everyone in your family. No one knew where you were."

"Hiding right beneath your nose," she answered.

"I've been worried sick."

"I took no risks. I kept all my doctor appointments. Your family has been really good to me."

He felt another lance of pain. "I should have been the one taking good care of you."

"I don't think we belong together—"

"But we do," he interrupted quietly, firmly. "I haven't expressed my feelings properly, and I apologize, and vow to become better, and more communicative, but you must know that just because I struggle with words, doesn't mean I don't feel, and don't care. Charlotte, I love you. I care for you so much that I can't imagine a future without you in it. I don't want a future without you in it. You are my future."

Her head turned and she looked up at him, her eyes slowly filling with tears. "You have your son now. You don't need me. I did my job. I gave you what you wanted. Now I just want you to let me go."

"*Cara*, baby."

The tears shimmered in her eyes, turning the blue irises aqua. "I can't live like this anymore." Her eyes closed, and a tear spilled. "I don't want to live like this. Let me go."

"I love you, Charlotte."

"Don't lie to me."

He bent over her and wiped away the tear before kissing her near the corner of her mouth. Her lips trembled. "I love you, Charlotte."

Another tear slipped free. He wiped that one, too. "I love you, Charlotte," he repeated.

"They're just words."

"But they're the words you needed to hear, and

I should have told you. I should have said them before, not just once, but over and over, until you felt safe, and loved. Because you are loved. You are my heart, Charlotte. Come back to me. Stay with me. Give me a chance to show you I'm the one for you."

Her mouth quivered as she gave her head a faint shake. "I can't do more pain."

"There's no more pain. We've done that part already. It's time for happiness. Time for love. Time for change. I promise. I swear. I give you my word."

Her eyes slowly opened and she looked at him. "I don't want your word. I want your heart."

"You have it, *cara*. You have all of it."

"Why do you feel now, but you didn't before?"

He used the pad of his thumb to dry her cheek. "I feel. I've always felt things, sometimes so strongly that I keep those emotions under lock and key."

"Why?"

He shrugged. "I was the youngest in a big family. Everyone else was important. Everyone else had a voice. I was the baby, dismissed as shallow and silly, a boy with a pretty face. I learned to hide things, especially the things that affected me deeply. It's become a terrible habit, and I promise to never again shut you out."

Her hand reached for his. Her fingers circled his. "I need to know how you feel. We need to know, your baby and me."

"Our baby," he corrected. "And, yes, I agree."

CHAPTER ELEVEN

IT WAS A week before she was released from the hospital but now they were all back at the *castello*, a family having come home.

The grapes were close to being harvested, and the days were long and warm. During the morning and early afternoon, Brando was in the fields, and with his winemakers, but late afternoon he always returned to her. Now Charlotte drowsed in the lounge chair beneath an umbrella by the pool, their newborn asleep on her chest, while Brando swam laps. She could hear the lazy hum of bees in the flowers in the big terra-cotta pots and the warble of a distant bird. Now and then she opened her eyes to watch him swim, marveling at the ripple of bronzed skin and muscle against the sparkling water.

He was magnificent.

And he was hers.

Finally.

The baby stirred against her and Charlotte nuzzled him even as she rubbed his tiny back. He smelled heavenly. Of milk. And love. He was so very loved.

"You know, we really need to give him a name," Charlotte said as Brando climbed from the pool before wrapping a towel around his lean waist. "We can't just call him 'the baby' forever."

"Why not?" Brando retorted, leaning over them, to drop a kiss on her mouth and then on the back of his son's head. "I was called 'baby' for years in my family."

She laughed softly, appreciating his humor. Brando grinned down at her, white teeth flashing, silver eyes filled with warmth.

"Aren't we supposed to name him after one of your father's brothers or something?" she asked. "Remind me again of the Italian tradition? I find it very confusing."

"Don't worry about the tradition. I don't think we need to follow any rules. We should give him a name that we think will suit him, a strong male name, as he's a strong boy."

"A miracle boy. He was determined to come into the world."

Brando nodded. "Determined to be made."

Her heart turned over. "Determined to bring us together."

Brando crouched next to them and kissed her again. "And he did. Our miracle. Our angel."

Charlotte's eyes met his. "Angel. Angelo."

Brando was silent a moment and then kissed her, and then the baby's cheek. "We love you, our Angelo."

Charlotte's heart was so full. She blinked back tears as she reached up to caress Brando's hard, chiseled jaw. "And I adore you, Brando. Thank you for loving me. Thank you for giving me this amazing family."

"And thank you, *cara*, for being mine. I love you."

"I know." And she did.

EPILOGUE

September, two years later

IT WAS HARVEST season and life at the *castello* was unusually busy, with two babies and a very busy husband who spent more time in the vineyards than he did at the house, but Charlotte understood and was almost as excited as Brando about this year's harvest.

After feeding the newest addition to the family, another boy, seven-month-old Joseph, Charlotte left the contented babies in care of their day nanny, and put on a hat, and left the house in search of her missing husband.

She hadn't gotten very far before she saw him approaching. He was on his way back to the *castello*, his white shirt damp and sticking to the hard planes of his chest.

He smiled when he spotted her. "Where are you going?"

"I was looking for you."

"Is everything all right?"

"Everything's perfect, and I thought maybe, just maybe, I could steal you away from work… But only if you've time."

"It depends on why I'm needed."

She loved the teasing light in his silver eyes and the husky note in his voice. Everything about him was so impossibly sexy. "I've had lots of time with the children, but I could use some adult time." She gave him a pointed look. "I could use some of you."

His smile widened, and he lowered his head to drop a warm, melting kiss on her lips. The kiss was full of promise and she pressed herself closer to him, desire flaring, hot and hungry. "You can use me all you want," he said against her mouth.

"Good. I intend to."

Brando wrapped an arm around her, holding her firmly to his chest and hips. She could feel the hard ridge of his erection through his work jeans, the ridge of his shaft rubbing her right where she was sensitive. "You still make me crazy," she whispered, arching against him, wanting all of him. "You make me want you morning, noon and night."

"Which is probably why we have a second baby already."

She smiled. "I have a feeling we're going to end up with a big family."

"As long as there are no more difficult pregnancies, I'm good with that."

"Last one was easy."

"Yes, it was. Thank you, Joseph." Brando swung her into his arms and cut across the gravel path, making a swift detour to the gated swimming pool.

She hummed with excitement and that electric heat that always crackled between them. "Where are you taking me?" she asked.

"Somewhere we can get some privacy." He pushed open the gate, and carried her into the pool house, and locked the door behind them.

The shutters were closed and the inside of the small stone building was dark and cool, smelling of lavender and citrus. Brando stripped Charlotte's clothes off and walked her backward to the oversize chaise, before nudging her down. He dropped to his knees, and kissed her right knee, and then the left, and then higher, up her tense thigh.

She sighed his name, her breath no longer steady. He pressed between her thighs, parting them wider, making room for his body, but instead of filling her, he kissed her, there where she was so wet and tender, where every flick of his tongue created licks of fire. Her hips danced of their own volition, her body desperate for him. These kisses were maddening. His flicking tongue was maddening. What she wanted was the heavy weight of him, the consuming pleasure that only he could give her. She needed him, needed him desperately, now and forever.

Brando never tired of the taste of his Charlotte, or her soft urgent cries. He loved the feel of her in his arms, the silk of her pale gold hair, and the shimmer in her eyes as she reached for him. Her passion for him was matched only by his need for her. He loved how much of herself she gave, whether they were making love, or being a family. As he made love to her on the chaise, he didn't just give her his body, he was giving her his heart. Making love was more than sex, more than sensation. It was a pledge between them, to always put their love and family first.

Charlotte was still independent, and strong, but he'd come to understand that what she needed most was loyalty, commitment and stability. She needed hope and family. He wasn't perfect but he understood these things, and knew that this was a promise he could keep. To protect his Charlotte. To protect their children. They were his life now, and he cherished this life with them because it was full of hope, and love. Always love.

And maybe another baby.

* * * * *

Captivated by
The Price of a Dangerous Passion?
You won't be able to resist these other stories by Jane Porter!

Kidnapped for His Royal Duty
The Prince's Scandalous Wedding Vow
His Shock Marriage in Greece
Christmas Contract for His Cinderella

Available now!